THE
BITTER QUESTION

The Caver Gang Stories: Book One · A Bitter Verse Novel

THE BITTER QUESTION
The Bitter Verse:
The Caver Gang Stories Book 1

A Mythic Horror by Augustus Martis

Echoes of Service Publishing LLC

Indianapolis, Indiana

THE BITTER QUESTION:
THE CAVER GANG STORIES BOOK 1
A BITTER VERSE NOVEL

Echoes of Service Publishing LLC, Indianapolis, Indiana

Original cover design: @samstalgia
Release cover design: Damian Modena
Original logo design: @momojipeachi
Interior design & layout: Echoes of Service Publishing LLC

ISBN [Print]: 978-1-970000-01-6
ISBN [E-book]: 978-1-970000-00-9

For rights, representation, or publishing inquiries, please contact:
Echoes of Service Publishing LLC
www.eospublishingllc.com

DEDICATED TO...

EVERY WRITER WHO
DREAMED OF ONE DAY BEING
AN AUTHOR.

IF I CAN DO IT, SO CAN YOU.

KEEP IMAGINING.

KEEP WORLDBUILDING.

KEEP WRITING

"I will share no secrets of the Caver Gang
with anyone outside our coven.

I will defend the honor of all Caver Gang
members: past, present, and future.

I will cause no harm to another Caver unless
it is to save them from harm.

I will ensure my position as a Caver is filled
by one of the future generations."

— *The Caver Oaths, as sworn and remembered*

TABLE OF CONTENTS

PART II — "...BUT FIVE COINS CAN CHANGE IT."

Author's Foreword

I am still blinking at the screen, half expecting someone to lean over my shoulder and say, *"Nice mock-up. Now where is the real book?"* Yet here we are. My first novel has been loosed into the wild. I have been chasing stories since I was twelve, filling spiral notebooks under the mattress and sneaking fanfiction onto classroom computers, but I never imagined that getting published would actually happen one day.

Those early pages were thin reflections of whatever worlds I had just inhaled. When I first picked up *The Lightning Thief*, Rick Riordan showed me that mythology could wear sneakers and crack jokes. Patrick Rothfuss proved to me that prose could sing without losing its bite, so much so that his words are tattooed upon my shoulder. Brandon Sanderson, with his clockwork magic systems, handed me the blueprints for building a universe that actually holds together and runs smoothly. Their shelves became my syllabus, their craft the permission slip I needed to try harder to become the best writer I could be. I can only dream that one day they may read this and know how much their works have inspired me.

Life, being far less tidy than a three-act structure, swept me out to sea. I enlisted in the United States Navy and traded lore and worldbuilding for nuclear reactors and Sea trials. Shipboard nights were loud and endless, but I never had trouble imagining new stories when underway. When a medical discharge sent me home sooner than planned, life demanded many things, and writing had to take even more of a backseat.

If you are reading this foreword, you are about to step into a world where memory is currency, divinity decays, and a single whispered choice can splinter a life. I cannot promise safe passage; my narrator has pried up floorboards best left unbothered. I can promise honesty. Every page carries fingerprints from the kid who wrote terrible *Dragonball Z* fanfiction on his old PC, the sailor who learned that storms can be calmer than home during shore leave, and the veteran piecing together what comes after duty ends and your body betrays you.

As for the story of this story, it began after my fourth back surgery. I had a moment of clarity while I was laid up on my couch, buzzing with painkillers, and listening to the newest episode of CreepCast covering the story 'Tales from the Gas Station'. The Bitter Verse began to bubble up on that blank-white, sedative laced afternoon.

So, my first thanks must go out to Isaiah Markin and Hunter Hancock, the hosts of CreepCast. Thank you so much for inspiring me down this path. And to all the loyal Creeps out there who spent late-nights wondering if they should finally write something, in the immortal words of Shia LaBeouf, ***"Just Do It!"***

The earliest version of this story surfaced on r/DeepNightSociety, a corner of Reddit lit by the flashlight glares of horror-seekers. Each of their beams highlight a tale from a struggling author that is trying to make their way in the sea of nightmare-inducing-tales. If you enjoy this book, and are eagerly awaiting for the next, consider checking them out.

So, I dug down into the soil of my imagination, pulled up a nugget of a story, took a deep breath, and tossed it into those dark depths. I was certain it would sink to the bottom and be forgotten.

But, instead, readers hauled it up and looked at it closer than I could have hoped. They were excited by the potential in that ore and asked for more pieces. For a whole story forged of its metal. And just for them, I mined out more of the raw material and found the elements that would soon become *The Bitter Question.* For that, I owe thanks to r/DeepNightSociety and all its readers.

Once I had all the ore I could find, I melted it all down and made it into a dull-ingot of a novel. It was only with the help of my alpha and beta-readers, who kept the forge hot, that I was able to make that lackluster chunk of a tale. Thank you all so much, I never would've gotten this far without your excitement.

The Bitter Question truly took on color when @samstalgia dropped a piece of fan art. Seeing my characters rendered by another hand felt like meeting them for the first time. Sam's art graced the original e-book's cover, and their enthusiasm reminded me that stories are more like invitations into a world than they are declarations of what is in that world. Thank you so much Sam, your talents are so much more precious than you realize.

I self-published that story with little hope of it ever gaining traction. But someone took interest in it and wanted to sell that story to a wider audience. So, I polished that chunk of processed narrative into the story you now hold. For that, I owe James Hettinger a good bottle of his favorite spirits and a heartfelt thank you. You truly made a lifelong dream come true.

But there are a few others that I also owe direct thanks to.

First is Chris Eggbert; he endured countless games of *Apex Legends* while I refused to shut up about this story. And yet, he was also excited for every part of the story being dropped on Reddit, and for that I'm thankful.

To Anthony Dubé-Leblanc, you disgusting Frenchman, thank you for always helping me worldbuild and bounce ideas off of you. I know you will help more than anyone else as I craft more of The Bitter Verse in the future. You really are the best friend a writer could ask for.

Lastly, but definitely not least, is Travis Kuhlman. I am often the mentor or wizened friend for those young writers around me seeking guidance. Tavis is the one writer-friend that I felt comfortable to lean on when I doubted myself and needed reassurance. As I often say, *"What a homie"*, and boy what a homie he is. Thanks man.

But most of all, thank you dear reader. Thank you for trusting me with a sliver of your time. Remember, sometimes the cost of an answer is more than the coins you pay for it. And may the Bitter Verse echo in your mind long after you turn the final page.

— Augustus Martis

October 2025

Preface

Some names and details have been changed to protect the people involved. I'm sure if I had a lawyer, they would tell me to say that this is a work of fiction, that nothing here is legally binding. That it isn't an admission of guilt.

But it's not a lie, either. And it's not an apology. Not really. There's no version of this story where I come out looking like the good guy. No, this is just an explanation. So...

To Allen: I'm sorry I made you my accomplice and called it loyalty. I asked you to keep quiet, hid in your house, and let you carry my bottles and my silence. Thank you.

To Theo: I used you as my conscience when I couldn't find my own. You forced me to remain when I tried to disappear, and I never did the same for you. I'm sorry.

To Shannon: I never truly understood you, and I didn't try. In your basement, I should have told you the truth... If I was scratched, I hope it was you that did it.

To Alicia: You carried the best and worst of me, and never complained. But I saw it, the moment when the love left your eyes. I understand, though. You always deserved better than what I gave you.

I'm sorry we asked. You didn't know what it would cost. You thought it would hurt, but then give you control. Instead, it hollowed you out and made you into something you'd hate. We didn't become someone better. We just became what was left.

I don't expect any of you to forgive me. But if there's any hope in this telling, it's that maybe now you will all understand why I did everything and then ran away.

But if you, my dear reader, have managed to read this and remember it... Please—I beg you—make sure it finds its way to them. They deserve to know at least.

Alright. Let's get to it.

-W.

Three Coins Will Buy You An Answer...

THREE COINS FROM YOUR POCKET

WILL BUY YOU AN ANSWER:

ONE COIN FREELY GIFTED

ONE MADE IN A BARGAIN

AND ONE WRONGLY LIFTED

Chapter 1
The First Domino

It was the sticky-hot July of 2001, and I had just finished eighth grade — thirteen years old, stuck in that strange, weightless space between childhood and whatever came next — when my dad got a job offer too good to turn down. So, we packed up everything we owned and moved across Tennessee, leaving behind our old lives: a Copperhead shedding its skin, easy, quiet, and unaware of what still clings underneath. It felt like a chance to start over. And, for a little while, it was.

Most kids my age would've been upset at the sudden move, but I wasn't bothered at all. Actually, I was quite excited by the prospect of a fresh start.

My birthday fell in September, meaning I was always the youngest kid in my class. On top of that, I was always on the heavier side, and was made fun of for it. I had no friends to speak of and was generally the punch line of every interaction I had.

However, in the middle of eighth grade, puberty hit me, a freight train carrying voice cracks, uncomfortable hair growth, and a wealth of emotions I was far too unprepared for. I slimmed up drastically and grew to be five feet eight inches tall over a short three-month period, so I took this move as a chance to reinvent myself.

As my dad drove down the interstate I cleared my throat,

making sure my voice wouldn't crack, and said, "I'm going to go by Will from now on."

It was one of my middle names, and I had decided to use it to make a clean break from the child I was leaving behind. My mom turned around in her seat to look at me, studying me for a moment before glancing at my dad. He kept his eyes on the road but gave a single stern nod, the kind that held more weight than it let on.

My mom gave a weak smile. The kind of smile that tries to hide disappointment. "Okay baby, if that's what you want." She still called me that, *baby*, as if she held onto the hope that it could keep me from growing up too fast.

Out the window, the landscape was already starting to change. The wide, open farmland of Middle Tennessee gave way to denser woods and low, rising hills: the ground itself drawing in tighter, folding up into something older and harder to read. The land wasn't the only thing that felt like it had curled in on itself.

The town we were moving to had maybe two thousand people on a good day and more gravestones whispering from its woods than living neighbors. It felt like a place that had died but kept walking, a ghost pretending to be a suburb and population hub six exits down I-40.

It wasn't always like that. Before the interstate bled it dry, the town's stubborn pride clung to the bustling depot at its heart. Now the rusted tracks still peek through choking weeds, a boarded-up station standing like a memory of purpose lost. Most folks drive off each morning down that same highway, trading empty roads and decaying pride for jobs in the city beyond.

The small neighborhood that held our new house was made up of two roads with a smaller road connecting the two, making a rough 'H' shape. Where the bottom of the "H" connected to the main road of the town, the top points dead-ended into the deep woods that surrounded the neighborhood, roads holding a breath for an expansion that never came. Our house sat in the right-bottom corner of the letter, and from the driveway we could see all of the connecting road and part of the opposite street.

Across that opposite street was an empty lot, about half the size of a football field, with grass that looked clean-cut and well maintained. As we unloaded the moving truck, I noticed a group of kids riding their bikes into the field. They lingered for a bit, watching us while more trickled in. When the last few arrived, they split into two teams and started a game of tag football.

I did my best not to stare, like that might make me seem cooler, like someone who'd seen groups like that before. But my mom noticed anyway and sent me off to introduce myself, making me promise to be back before dinner. I agreed and hurried across the street to meet them.

There were eleven of them in the field when I walked up. They stopped mid-play, the ball bouncing to a stop as they all turned and watched me, a rare bird they'd never seen before.

A boy about my size stepped forward with a kind of swagger that felt practiced. He had a mop of chestnut-brown hair that looked like it had been combed with his fingers, and a faint shadow of a mustache that didn't quite commit to growing in. He wore a sleeveless tee with faded lettering across the chest and cargo shorts that hung a little too low on his hips, an awkward reach toward adulthood.

He ran a hand through his hair and smirked like he'd been waiting his whole life to use this moment.

"Welcome to the neighborhood," he said, trying to make his voice sound an octave lower than it probably was.

I nodded, trying not to look nervous. "Thanks. You guys need another player?"

"Yeah, I was getting tired of being 'Always QB' anyway." He stuck out a hand. "Name's Allen. What's yours?"

"J…Will," I said, catching myself before I said the name I'd been trying to leave behind.

Allen grinned and gave my hand a quick shake before turning to the rest of the kids. "Let's introduce you to the gang."

I followed his gestures as he pointed around the group, but I barely took in most of the names. My eyes caught on her.

I didn't know how I hadn't noticed her right away. She stood a little off to the side, arms crossed, eyes sharp. She didn't look at me; she looked through me, judging and measuring.

She had red hair pulled back in a messy ponytail, a few strands falling out to frame her freckled face. Her tank top showed strong shoulders and pale skin, and my eyes were immediately drawn to the curve of her neck, the shape of her arms, the way she held herself, a girl who feared nothing. She didn't seem shy or silly; she just stood there, calm and confident, a grown-up pretending to be a teenager.

I'd never seen a girl like her before.

She couldn't have been more than a year or two older than me, maybe fourteen or fifteen, but in my head, she filled the room. The embodiment of a real teenager. Not like Allen, who tried to act older and cooler but was clearly still a boy. She didn't try to seem older. She just was.

I didn't know what made her feel so different. I just knew I wanted her to notice me.

Allen kept rattling off names, Kelly and Luke, eight-year-old twins, plus a couple of kids I figured were in middle school like me. They all seemed friendly enough, but I didn't remember half their names by the time the game restarted. My focus kept drifting back to the redhead.

"Shannon," Allen said finally, nodding toward her. "She's my sister. Step-sister, but we've lived together since we were little, so, y'know."

She gave me a single glance, a flicker barely more than a blink, then looked away.

She didn't smile. That should have made me nervous. Instead, it made me want to impress her.

The game picked back up, and I joined in without needing to be asked again. My hands were shaking a little the first time the ball was thrown to me, but I caught it. Allen gave a celebratory shout, and someone, I think Luke, yelled that I was "actually pretty fast."

Between plays, the kids started asking me questions: where I came from, what games I liked, if I had a bike. I tried to answer casually, but I kept sneaking glances at Shannon, watching the way her ponytail bounced as she ran, the way she ducked her shoulder when she tagged people out, the way she managed to catch me by surprise twice.

Once, when I was chasing her, I noticed two little black dots on the back of her left shoulder, perfectly round, a couple of inches apart. I thought they might be fake tattoos or weird freckles. I didn't ask; I didn't want to sound stupid.

Eventually, a sharp honk echoed from my driveway. The sun was getting lower and deepening to the bloody hue of cheap, rusted metal. The dusk settled heavy and hushed, as if it knew something I didn't. My mom's silhouette waved from the back porch that faced the field.

"I gotta go," I called out, panting. "Mom wants me home before dinner."

"Are we playing tomorrow?" I added quickly, trying my best not to sound overeager.

Allen looked like he was about to say yes but paused. He turned to Shannon. Their eyes met; a whole conversation seemed to pass between them in silence. She didn't speak but gave the smallest shrug, as if she were tired of arguing.

Allen smiled and turned back to me. "Yeah. Something different though."

He clapped me on the back, draped an arm around my shoulders like we were already friends, and walked me toward the street. "Bring a bottle of water and wear some old jeans. Trust me."

"I'll be here," I promised, then glanced over my shoulder one last time.

Shannon was still watching me.

I wasn't sure what she saw. But I knew I wanted her to keep looking.

When I got home, I sat down with my parents in the living room around a bucket of fried chicken my mom had picked up for dinner. I told them about the group of kids and got permission to meet up with them the next day.

After dinner I went down the stairs to my new 'rooms.' The house had a finished basement with its own den, bathroom, and bedroom. The den had a bar and a built-in entertainment center, which my dad promised to set up with my PlayStation and a new TV so I wouldn't have to use the one upstairs. The bathroom had a sink, toilet, and standing shower, and my mom said I could decorate it "within reason", which meant she'd pick everything herself. The bedroom already held my full-size bed, dresser, and desk, with room to spare.

And it was all mine.

Going from a tiny bedroom with barely enough space for my twin-size bed and dresser to practically a condo was amazing.

The house seemed warm and full, a place where things might finally go right. I slept soundly, a rock unaware that the next day would be the first domino to topple in the horrifying Rube Goldberg Machine of my life.

Chapter 2
Beginners Maw

I scarfed down the two PB&Js my mom made for lunch and washed them down with an orange-flavored Mountain Dew, whatever chemical brew passed for citrus that day. I emptied my plain black backpack, stuffed it with a few bottles of water and more Mt. Dews, and headed for the front door.

"Here," Mom said, using that light "don't-push-me" tone, she saved for curfews and unfinished homework. She pressed a cheap Velcro-strapped wristwatch into my palm; the kind sold from a fishbowl on a gas-station counter. The nylon band smelled faintly of her lemon dish soap; she must have wiped it clean first.

"I already set the alarm for five," she added, tapping the scratched plastic face like she was fastening the rule in place. "Home by six. Got it?" She never said why six p.m. mattered, only that anything later felt like tempting fate, which I never understood at the time.

"Yes ma'am."

"Be safe. Love you."

"Love you too."

I buckled the watch, noting how loose the strap felt compared to the ones I had lost or broken over the years. Mom kept replacing them as if each new timepiece might finally keep me anchored to her sense of order. The thought warmed me more than the soda had.

I stepped outside. The air felt heavier than it had that morning, humid and still, as if the day held its breath. I followed the connecting street back to the field where four shapes waited at the tree line. I recognized two of them right away.

Allen spotted me first and grinned like he'd been expecting me. He broke from the group with easy swagger. Shannon didn't move, just kept her cold green eyes pinned to me like I'd shown up late to something unspoken. She looked annoyed, maybe bored, maybe something else. Whatever it was, she clearly wasn't happy to see me.

Beside her stood a shorter, compact boy built like a pitbull, and a tall girl with enough presence to outsize them all. They both looked to be around Allen and Shannon's age.

"Will!" Allen called. "Perfect timing, dude. Lemme introduce you to the rest of the Caver Gang. This is Alicia and Theo."

Alicia offered a small, cautious wave from her spot, not lifting her hand past her shoulder. Shannon was the kind of girl you got in trouble for staring at; Alicia, the kind who could spike a volleyball through your chest. She was tall, taller than anyone else there, and built with the kind of legs and shoulders that made you think of gym class and dodgeball-patterned bruises.

At the time, I thought of her as the athletic type, like that made her less confusing than Shannon somehow. But that was just thirteen-year-old logic, trying to sort girls into types I didn't understand yet.

What actually caught my attention wasn't her height or lingering air of strength. It was the way the jaw length cloud of oak-colored curls bounced when she moved, and how the sun caught warm, reddish tones in her hair that didn't seem to be there in the shadows. Her smile was small and uncertain, but it stuck with me longer than it had any right to.

Theo, on the other hand, didn't wait for an introduction. He rushed forward and threw his arms around me in a bear hug so sudden it nearly knocked the breath out of me. He didn't even reach my chin, but he was thick with muscle, solid and coiled. He had the perfect build for a wrestler and easily outweighed me by twenty-five pounds despite being a solid half-foot shorter than me.

The hug was tight, but careful. Controlled. Even then I remember thinking, *This guy is used to holding things back*. I had no doubt he could've snapped me in half without much effort.

He wore a sleeveless shirt that showed off just how well puberty had been treating him, even while denying him the height that was so cherished by teenage boys. His skin was darker than mine, smooth over his arms but speckled with acne along his jaw. Even so, he probably would've been considered better looking than me or Allen by most girls our age, though I wouldn't have admitted that out loud.

When he pulled back, he gave me a once-over and nodded like he was appraising livestock.

"Oh yeah," Theo said with a grin. "He'll fit just fine."

"Fit?" I asked, raising an eyebrow at Allen. "What is he talking about?"

"Beginner's Maw," Alicia muttered, then reached out and gave Allen a half-hearted slap on the arm. The motion looked awkward, like she wasn't used to faking anger. "You didn't tell him what we were doing, you ass?"

Allen yelped dramatically and rubbed at his wounded arm. "Of course not! No one told me before I went in, either."

Theo nodded solemnly and stroked his chin like a kung-fu movie sensei. "That's right. We didn't. Maybe it's better this way, keep the kids in the dark."

"What's a 'Beginner's Maw'?" I asked, trying not to let the name sound as ominous as it felt.

"It's—" Alicia started, but Theo cut her off with both hands in the air.

"No, no, no! Let him find out when we get there. I like this new approach."

Allen grinned, threw an arm around my shoulder like we were already blood brothers, and steered me away from the group, not toward the street, but toward the shadowed edge of the woods.

Like the entire neighborhood, the back of the field was lined by woods, with foliage thick enough that the midday summer heat noticeably cooled as we broke into the shade. The ground was covered in twigs and branches from countless spring and autumn storms. A clear path wound through the trees, worn by teenagers who came before.

As I followed behind Theo I noticed a pair of black dots on the top of his right shoulder near the outer arm. They matched the pair on Shannon's left shoulder perfectly in size and distance apart. I wanted to ask about them, but it felt too awkward to bring up suddenly.

We chatted about pointless things as we wove through the woods and soon the sound of a creek joined our idle banter. We came up on the running water moments later, which was much wider than I had guessed from the sound.

"Alright, here's Shit Creek," Allen said as he walked down to the edge and dipped his fingers in.

"Shit Creek? Really?"

"That's what everyone calls it, since it feeds into the water-processing plant for the county," Alicia offered with a shrug. "It flows into a bigger river the next county over. High schoolers meet farther upstream on weekends to party. You need four-wheelers or dirt bikes to get there, though."

"But that's not what we are here for," Theo said, already moving upstream along the gravel band that passed for a path. "It's a bit further. Keep up."

Shannon's gaze tracked me the whole time, chin tucked, shoulders pitched forward like she was bracing for an impact only she could feel.

"We already have a full headcount," she muttered just loud enough for me to hear, kicking a clod of mud as she passed it. Allen tried for a joke, but she cut him off. "Not every stray needs a pack, Allen. We're doing fine."

The words landed light yet sharp, a warning rather than a snarl. Underneath it I caught the flicker of something raw, hurt dressed up as caution, then the mask slid back into place.

Allen fell into step beside me and bumped my elbow, hoping that I hadn't heard her. "First time I did this walk I tried to act cool and slipped on a wet root. Theo swears I screamed."

"I did not swear," Theo called without turning. "I stated a historic fact."

Alicia snorted and adjusted the strap of her small pack. "You squeaked, Allen. Like a hamster that found out that hamster-Jesus had abandoned the world."

"More like he found out the chipmunk heathens were right and that hamster-Jesus was never real," Theo threw back over his shoulder.

Allen clutched his heart and staggered in mock pain. When the playful groan faded, he leaned closer, voice dropping to a conspiratorial murmur only I could hear.

"Don't let them fool you. They roast everyone on their first trek. Comes with the territory." He nodded toward the trees. "Tradition number one: every rookie has to pick a trail name after the first successful crawl. Something embarrassing if you let them choose, so think ahead."

"Trail name?" I asked. "Like a call sign?"

"Exactly. Theo was 'Mud Monster' for a year because he fell face first into the creek. Alicia is 'Spike' for clocking me with a volleyball. Shannon… well, she never tells hers, which somehow makes it worse. You survive Beginner's Maw; you'll probably be assigned one of your own soon enough."

Before I could answer, Alicia's voice cut in from a few steps ahead. "Allen, stop scaring the kid with your made-up bylaws."

"Made up? Name one that isn't real."

She shrugged without turning. "The mud face-paint ceremony. You invented that on the walk last summer."

"Traditions have to start somewhere," he called back, defensive but smiling.

I laughed a little too loudly. The sound felt strange, like I had borrowed it from someone more at ease with the world.

Shannon brought up the rear, silent but not disconnected. She flicked small stones into the creek as we walked, each pebble hitting a ripple with a neat plink. Every so often I caught her eyes on me, measuring, weighing, then drifting away again.

We followed the water for about ten minutes, shoes sliding on damp moss when the bank narrowed. Conversation rose and fell in easy waves: Theo pointing out raccoon tracks, Alicia guessing the water temperature, Allen telling a story about a middle-school dance disaster that made everyone groan. I answered when asked, listened more than I spoke, and tried to pin their voices to memories, afraid I'd mix them up later.

When the trees widened around a bend, the creek gave up its secret.

The Rock waited, a pale block of limestone jutting over the current, a careless giant's dropped stone. The water curled around the slab, slow and respectful, convinced the stone had every right to be exactly where it was.

"You remembered a bottle, right?" Allen's voice carried a jitter of excitement.

I unzipped my pack and held up two.

"Oh, rookie over-prepared." He grinned. "You only need one, and it has to be empty."

I drank from the first, poured the rest into the creek.

"Anything else?"

"Leave your pack and follow us," Shannon said. She dropped her satchel beside a tree, the gesture brisk, and I mirrored her.

Twenty yards beyond The Rock, a scar in the hillside

appeared.

Beginner's Maw.

It looked less like a mouth, more like a wound, a horizontal gash maybe twenty feet wide and four feet high. The same giant who lost the limestone block might have dragged a shovel across the slope and never bothered to patch the damage. Time remembered even if people had forgotten.

Theo's voice settled into something part ceremony, part dare. "Allen nominated you. You crawl in, fill the bottle, drink the water on top of The Rock, carve your name, done. After that we can take you to the Ora—"

Shannon slapped his arm, a sharp crack that bounced off the trunks. Theo towered over her, yet he only rubbed the spot and held his tongue.

"Not yet," she said. She pointed into the dark seam. "He earns it first."

I faced the opening, trying to read its depth from the black. "How far does it go?"

"You'll find that out yourself," Allen answered. His voice carried a mock gravity, corners of his mouth twitching upward.

Theo stepped in beside him and lowered his voice so only I could hear. "First time's rough for everybody," he said. "I got stuck in that squeeze right there and scraped half the skin off my elbow trying to wriggle backward. Thought the cave was gonna keep me." He let out a short laugh, more amused than embarrassed. "Allen dragged me out, patched me up, and shoved me right back in. Point is, you just keep moving and remember to breathe. Cave only wins if you quit."

The story shouldn't have helped, but it did. If Theo could mess up that badly and still come out smiling, maybe I could survive one crawl.

I slid the empty bottle into my back pocket and drew a breath that tasted of wet leaves. Four friends, new friends, waited behind me like it was Wednesday, and caves were ordinary. If they could do it, so could I.

"See you on the other side," I said, trying to sound braver than I felt, and dropped to my knees at the edge of the dark.

And yet, staring into that slit of darkness, I felt a wave of panic rise in my chest. I did not let it build. I did not let it name itself. I just moved.

The entrance was easy enough. I had to duck a little to walk upright toward the back. About ten yards in, the cave began to narrow, both in width and height, like a throat. The name started to make more sense.

To keep going, I had to drop to my hands and knees.

I glanced back once. The silhouettes of the Caver Gang stood just outside the light, watching. Waiting.

Not wanting to look scared, I dropped down and crawled forward.

Soon I was in total darkness. True darkness. It wasn't the weak black of night or my room deep within my basement. Those places still offer a hint of something: the faint glow of moonlight through curtains, the distant smear of a streetlamp, the ghost outline of furniture proving the world is still there. Here, there was nothing. No shapes, no half-shades, not even shadows. The dark felt solid, a velvet curtain pressed against my face, swallowing every stray glimmer of light.

That did not make it hostile. It was a fact of nature, the stone and earth whispering, *You belong to the light, and there is no light here. That is the way of things.*

My heart pounded louder with every breath, yet the thought of crawling back out empty-handed, only to be mocked for it, was stronger than this absolute darkness. So, I kept going.

The cave walls pulsed with slow rhythms, narrowing and widening like the flex of some ancient muscle. Every few feet the floor dipped lower. If the rocks had been slicker, I could have slid.

The ceiling dropped again, just enough to force a choice. No more crawling on hands and knees. I had to bellycrawl the rest of the way, so I did.

I was a newborn snake, still figuring out how to shift my weight without grinding myself into stone. I lifted one leg slowly, careful not to jab it against the jagged rock. Once it was parallel with my side, I reached ahead with the opposite hand, feeling for purchase in the dark, then pushed with the leg, hauled with the hand, and slid forward.

Push, pull, slide, breathe in the thick damp smell-taste of wet rock. Repetition wore me down. My shoulders throbbed, my thighs burned, and the skin of my stomach went numb against the chilled limestone.

Halfway through a drag the truth struck me: turning around would be impossible. Panic punched the air from my lungs. I pressed my cheek to the stone, counted five breaths, made myself believe I still owned them, then inched on.

I crawled another yard when a tickle of sound brushed my

right ear – a faint whisper that wasn't mine, a single sigh echoing through the squeeze. I froze, cheek pressed to the cold limestone. My pulse hammered in my ears as I held my breath, straining to listen. Was that… a voice? Nothing now but silence and my own heart knocking against stone. Just my mind playing tricks, I told myself fiercely. Gritting my teeth, I shoved myself forward again.

Ahead, a faint trickle of water threaded through the silence. The crawl had a destination. Panic loosened its grip. First a little, then enough that I noticed other things: the ghost taste of minerals in the air, the way my heartbeat thudded back from the walls, a second set of footsteps.

The tunnel stopped narrowing. I was not pinned, only held, stone on every side yet room enough to move. A few yards later the roof began to lift, first by inches, then by my full height. I stayed low, unwilling to test the darkness.

The whisper of water swelled. Six cautious shuffles and my hand plunged into a shallow pool so cold that it stung. I jerked back, heart hammering, then let out a bark of laughter that filled the hollow space. The sound came back warped and playful, as if the cave laughed too.

The knot in my spine uncoiled. Relief washed through me with a physical warmth, more startling than the water's chill. I cupped my hands, drank, tasted stone and iron and something older than either. In that taste I found a promise: deeper places waited, and I would not be satisfied until I met every one of them.

If I had to mark the moment caving claimed me, it was that laugh echoing off unseen walls, proof the dark could answer without malice.

Chapter 3
The Caver's Gulp

I filled the empty bottle with the water the best I could and turned back the way I came, making my way toward the entrance. The climb out was easier than the crawl in, and before long I saw the light of day.

But once I reached the mouth of the cave, I paused. The entrance was empty.

The goofy grin I'd been wearing since splashing my hand in the underground pool vanished, replaced by a creeping sense of dread. Had they left me? Had I taken too long? Was this part of the test? Had I already failed it?

I hurried toward the creek, scanning for signs of the others. Relief washed over me when I spotted the Caver Gang lounging around The Rock. Allen sat reclined against the stone, eyes closed, and face tipped toward the sun. Alicia and Shannon sat in the shallow edge of the creek, bare feet kicking gently through the current.

It was Theo, perched at the top of The Rock, who saw me first.

"Will! You look like shit, dude!" His voice boomed across the bend; all grin and zero malice. For the first time in a long while, someone laughing at me did not make me want to disappear.

I glanced down. My shirt and jeans were plastered with silty mud, and a thin ribbon of dried blood striped my forearm.

Theo vaulted from the slab and joined Allen. Alicia gasped and splashed toward me, her wet footsteps sharp against the hush of the creek. She reached me first, catching my elbow with surprising gentleness.

"Hold still a sec," she said, voice low, almost professional. She turned my arm so the cut faced the light. Her fingertips were cool and smelled faintly of river water and cheap watermelon lip-balm. A tiny crease formed between her brows.

She slid one of the spare water bottles from my pack, cracked it open, and poured a thin stream over the cut. Mud swirled away in rusty spirals. Then she dabbed the scrape with the cuff of her own sleeve, leaving a damp oval darker than the rest of the cotton.

I tried to joke. "Battle scars, right?" My voice cracked.

She didn't laugh, just offered a quick smile. "Scars are cooler when they don't get infected."

As she worked, I noticed freckles on her shoulders I had missed before, little constellations catching stray sun. Nobody outside my family had fussed over me like this since elementary scrapes. The care didn't feel like pity. It felt earned, somehow, like I had already proven a thing she valued.

Behind us, Shannon watched from the shallows. Her face remained unreadable, though one hand churned the water in slow, tight circles.

Alicia rinsed the cut once more, inspected it, then gave a satisfied nod. "Skin-deep. You'll live." She reached into the pocket of her shorts and pulled out a crumpled but unopened adhesive bandage. "Hold still." She tore the packet open with her teeth, smoothed the strip over the wound, and pressed the edges with her thumb. "There. Field medicine."

My chest felt weirdly light. "Thanks." The word seemed too small.

She shrugged. "Can't have you dripping all over The Rock."

Theo, now standing at the base of the slab, lifted a thumbs-up. "Nurse Alicia saves the day."

By the time she was finished fussing over the bandage, the others had gathered around The Rock, leaving a clear path up its gentle slope. Allen waited at the foot of that path, a rusted flat-head screwdriver in hand, grinning so wide it seemed his face had been waiting all afternoon for this single moment.

He pressed the tool into my palm, then gave my shoulder a quiet, reassuring squeeze that said plenty without needing words. For a second, with the fresh bandage snug against my arm and Allen's silent approval warm on my skin, I believed I might actually belong here.

With a nod, I tucked it into my back pocket next to the bottle of cave water and started the climb. Between the gentle incline and the clear divots for my hands and feet, it was almost as easy as climbing a ladder.

The top of The Rock was flatter than I expected and the only part in full sunlight. The limestone was warm to the touch, but nowhere near hot enough to burn. Years of rain had smoothed the stone but hadn't done much to erase the names carved into it. With a quick glance, I counted at least three hundred, and still plenty of room for hundreds more.

Once I got my footing, Theo cleared his throat and launched into a loud, official-sounding tone:

"As the longest-standing member, I call The Caver Gang to observe The Rite of Beginning for Will. We are gathered here today to accept a new member into our ranks. As stated by the rules, at least three current members are present to observe this sacred rite."

The cadence and wording made it obvious he'd memorized the script from some older kid years ago.

"Can anyone here deny that Will retrieved The Caver's Gulp on his own?"

Theo's question was met with a small chorus of nays from the group.

Alicia and Allen seemed fully invested in the moment, while Shannon casually examined her nails, picking at one with the other, a girl who had seen this all before.

"Will, the Caver Gang acknowledges that you have completed Beginner's Maw and retrieved the Caver's Gulp!"

All four made a guttural hoot, though one was noticeably half-hearted.

Theo continued with practiced authority: "By repeating the following oaths, do you swear to uphold them?"

I cleared my throat and nodded. "I swear."

"Repeat after me: I will share no secrets of the Caver Gang with anyone outside our coven."

"I will share no secrets of the Caver Gang with anyone outside our coven."

"I will defend the honor of all Caver Gang members: past, present, and future."

I repeated the words, standing a little taller, like they might grant me strength I hadn't earned yet.

"I will cause no harm to another Caver unless it is to save them from harm."

The weight of it sat heavy in my chest, but I said it anyway.

"I will ensure my position as a Caver is filled by one of the future generations."

That last part stuck with me, the idea that this thing had lasted for generations. Maybe that's how it kept going.

"Will, you have taken the Oaths. Drink now of your Caver's Gulp," Theo ordered with a thunderous clap of his hands. He clapped again, and this time the others joined in, their rhythm rough but steady.

I pulled out the bottle from my back pocket and looked at the surprisingly clear water I had collected. The 'Caver's Gulp' caught the light perfectly and scattered a splattered rainbow across the sunbaked stone, the pattern shifting in a slow, hypnotic wave as I tilted the bottle.

I twisted off the lid and took a deep drink of the mineral-flavored water, gulping down the entire half bottle.

They all clapped again, and this time none of them sounded bored with the ritual.

"Can anyone here deny that Will is now one of the Caver Gang?" Again, the chorus of nays replied. "Will, you may now add your name and this year to our sacred list of members."

I dropped to one knee and rubbed my hand across the surface, my fingers brushing over an assortment of names from the past: Ben '79; Jill '92; Luke '56; James 1924; Lacy '89. The last one was by far the most faded of the bunch.

At first, I was confused why Lacy's carving from the '80s looked more weathered than Luke's or James's. Then it hit me; it wasn't from the 1980s.

It was from the 1880s.

How long had the Caver Gang been around? It was hard to imagine.

With those thoughts of history and longevity in my mind, I was extra careful with my etching.

WILLIAM 2001

With that engraving, I was officially part of the Caver Gang.

Chapter 4
~~SCRATCHED~~

Once I stood back up, the others scrambled up The Rock and checked my handiwork. They took turns showing me their own names. All except Shannon.

Once I was sure she wasn't going to offer it freely, I turned to her and tilted my head slightly, "Where's yours?"

She gave me what was quickly becoming her trademark sigh and walked over to the edge that hung over the creek bend. She pointed down at the edge without saying anything. I walked to her spot and kneeled to look for her name.

"I don't see…?"

"It's over the edge," she said matter of factly.

I raised a brow in confusion. I went fully prone and slipped up to the edge so that I could look over it. There, upside down and shadowed from the sun, was her carving.

SHANNON '99

I noticed that there were only a handful of names carved over the edge like she had done. Once I stood up from the edge I blinked a bit, trying to word my question tactfully, "So, why over the edge?"

"She wanted to make sure it wouldn't fade as fast as all the ones on top," Allen said with an exaggerated roll of his eyes.

"I'm sorry," she bit back at him, "I take this shit seriously. I don't invite kids we just met to join us!" She toed one of the scratched-through names, digging a pebble into the groove. "Names are easy to carve," she said, barely above a whisper. "Keeping them safe is the hard part." She brushed grit from her fingertips and gave me a single, measuring look. It wasn't anger this time. It was just a wary promise that loose loyalty wouldn't survive here.

Suddenly the cold treatment she had been giving me so far made much more sense. She had been angry that Allen wanted me to join after just moving in, and was hoping that Theo or Alicia would stop the induction. When they had agreed, she was left with no recourse.

"Listen, Shannon, I didn't—" I started before she cut me off with a raised hand.

"It doesn't matter, it's done now. You are one of us," she said, closing the distance toward me with a raised index finger. Her finger met the center of my sternum, jabbing through my shirt, "What was your second oath, Will?"

I blinked at the question and did my best to remember the order of things I repeated, "To defend the honor of all Caver Gang members?" I flinched at the way I had said it: as a question instead of a statement.

"That's right, and do you know what that means?"

"That if someone is talking badly about one of us, I have to stand up for them?"

"That's riiight," she said with exaggerated claps, slow and mocking. "And what happens if you don't?"

"I… I broke my oath? I get kicked out? I don't know."

She stabbed her finger into my chest again, "It means you get 'scratched' and you are dead to us." She shifted her finger from my chest to point accusingly at the names carved below us. "Forever. Do you get that?"

I looked down at the surface and realized that some of the names, maybe one in twenty or thirty, had been scratched through at some point. Some were wide and messy, the name beneath completely unreadable with the marring. Like the person was never there, never existed. However, other cuts were *deep*. This left the name legible, so that all those who came after could know who they were and that they had betrayed the Cavers' oaths. A warning.

I looked at the other three members and none of them met my eyes. A chill crawled up my arms. If even Allen wouldn't look at me…

I finally looked back at Shannon and nodded solemnly to her question. "I get it."

Her eyes seemed to be watering slightly as they bounced back and forth between each of mine, looking for any weakness or deceit within them. When she didn't find any she huffed and turned away, descending The Rock to reclaim her spot at the water's edge. Alicia tossed me an apologetic look before following her down, laying an arm over Shannon's shoulder as the two whispered in hush tones.

"Ummm, sorry about that man," Theo said with a downturned look. "Come here, real quick." He guided me over to another corner and pointed at a carving.

~~AIDEN '99~~

I studied the name closely, rubbing my finger over it carefully. The scratch through the name was nearly twice as deep as the letters that they sought to destroy. This was a name someone wanted remembered as a traitor. I looked up at Allen who had joined us, "What happened?"

Allen sighed and looked away, leaving Theo to answer.

"Aiden was a guy from another neighborhood. There's a bunch of ways to get here, and the Caver Gang has a few different pockets of members. Typically, we'll meet other members here by chance and share any news. But most importantly we are all held to the same oaths.

"Shannon and Aiden started dating at the beginning of last school year. They got pretty serious. Well, they broke up at the beginning of summer because Aiden didn't want to be 'held down over the Summer.'"

"Is that why his name is scratched out?"

"No, no, that's not against the oaths. It's what he did after they broke up."

"He told everyone that he had taken her virginity and that they broke up because she was sleeping around with a bunch of high schoolers," Allen blurted out with a bark of angered laughter punctuating how absurd the claim was to him. There was an unbridled rage in his voice that I couldn't have imagined coming from the jovial teenager before that moment.

That's when it clicked, why she cared so much about the

second oath. Another Caver not only broke her heart, but also lied to hurt her reputation and honor. I looked down at the name and fought back the urge to scratch it even deeper.

"So even his neighborhood's pocket of members agreed to 'scratch' him?"

Theo sighed softly, "It was a little shaky at first, but Jordan, the oldest member of that group, believed us and Aiden was scratched."

I nodded and pointedly kicked across the surface of Aiden's name. I half climbed, half slid down The Rock and joined Alicia and Shannon, standing a few steps behind them.

"Hey, Shannon," I said, fighting back the wave of self-consciousness.

"What?" she asked without looking up from the creek. Alicia had dropped her arm away to look back at me, a look of caution plainly on her face.

"Tell me Aiden was a liar," I said.

In one motion she stood and whipped around, her glare was full of venom and daggers. A spike of nausea drove itself into my stomach. How did I expect this to play out? Why had I said that at all? Where had I gotten the courage to not only say his name to her, but to directly address the situation?

"Aiden is a fucking liar, and I hope he drowns in dicks until he chokes on one," she spat. Her cheeks were as red with anger as her eyes were from crying.

"Good," I said, spitting to the side. "He's dead to me and his name will never break my lips again."

Her eyes quickly went through a wave of different emotions:

doubt, curiosity, and finally belief.

"You swear?"

"I swear," I reassured her.

Alicia did her best to hide a smile, nodding to show her support of my conviction. Shannon wiped at her eyes once more and nodded, "Okay, fine."

We spent the remainder of the afternoon talking about other things, avoiding the topic that had almost ruined the entire day.

Theo, Shannon, and I were all going to be entering the ninth grade and joining Alicia and Allen at Upperpoint High School, where they would be advancing to tenth grade. The high school had just over eight hundred students, which was way more than the population of the town should've supported. However, since it was newer and nicer than the larger city's three different high schools, a lot of the families that lived outside the town or city chose to send their kids to Upperpoint.

Most Caver Gang ended up drifting away after getting their driver's licenses, but were still members that upheld their oaths. A lot of the teenagers that partied upstream of Shit Creek were members that aged up and still stayed close to their friends.

At some point in the string of conversations, I remembered that Theo had been stopped from sharing something by Shannon. I nudged him a bit and asked about what he was going to say.

"Oh, right, The Oracle," Theo said, rubbing the back of his head a bit. "It's something you'll have to experience for yourself, but we can take you there the day after tomorrow."

"Are you sure?" Alicia asked, blushing a bit for some reason.

"He's a Caver, he can go if he wants," Shannon said, her voice oddly guarded.

"He can brave the cave, that doesn't mean he has to…" Allen stopped himself from talking about me, turning to talk to me directly instead. "Well, you'll see when you get there."

I was going to press the topic, but my wristwatch began to beep loudly. I fumbled to turn off the alarm, "Shit, I gotta get home."

"Yeah, I'm pretty hungry too," Theo said, rubbing his stomach.

We all got our stuff together, made the trip back down the stream's bank, and through the woods to the field. We weren't all going to meet the next day, since Allen and Shannon had a family function and Theo had to go shopping with his mom for most of the day.

Alicia and I agreed to meet up the next day and she would take me around the neighborhood to show me where everyone lived.

We all split up and I headed home. My mom wasn't too pleased with how dirty my clothing had gotten, and made me take a shower before dinner. After cleaning up and putting a bandage on my arm I told my parents that I had met two new friends that day and was really fitting in, leaving out the detail that I had joined a group with the word 'gang' in their name.

Chapter 5
Fight the Flush

Alicia stopped her bike and pointed at another house, "That's where the twins live. We normally don't invite them to play in the field, but they show up most of the time anyway."

I pulled up next to her and looked at the small brick house with an appraising nod, "I can understand, they were a little hard to play with the other day."

She stretched her arms up and let out a bit of a yawn before looking up and down the street, "You wanna go lay in the field for a bit?"

I nodded and set off toward the field, weaving back and forth as she caught up. Once we reached the edge of the field, we dumped our bikes and walked to the back where the woods cast a cooling shadow over a few feet of the tampered grass.

As we got comfortable, I asked, "Who keeps the field trimmed and stuff?"

"Oh, my dad has been doing it since I asked two summers back," Alicia said with a shrug. She was an only child to a single father, and her house was the one directly next to the empty lot. She had mentioned at The Rock that her dad hadn't even been trying to date since her mom died five years ago.

"That's really cool of him," I said as I leaned back on my palms, watching the street with passive disinterest. A couple of the younger kids were riding their bikes back and forth, throwing glances at the two of us. "Say, what determines if you guys invite someone to join the Cavers?"

Alicia shrugged a bit, fully laying down with her hands entwined behind her head. She had closed her hazel eyes to the warm day. "I guess it's mostly based on how many are active and if we think we can trust them. Like, you know the kid with braces and black hair—Caleb? He's asked a ton of times to come with us, but we will probably never take him."

"How come?"

"He got caught trying to steal some Pokémon cards from another kid, so we can't trust him. That kind of stuff."

I felt a spike of self-consciousness, but needed to know. "Why was I invited so fast?"

"Allen said he had a good feeling about you."

"But why did you and Theo agree?"

There was a long moment of silence. Long enough for me to get curious and look over at her to see that she had opened her eyes to look at me. Once we locked eyes, she held my gaze for another long moment before closing her eyes once more, "Theo was a bit worried, but trusted Allen's gut feeling."

"And you?"

Another pause before she chuckled, "I thought you were cute, that's all."

I felt my face immediately flush and I quickly looked over at her in disbelief.

She was already wearing the biggest smile I'd ever seen on her face, having caught my panicked response. She laughed so hard that she rolled a bit side to side with the effort of the laugh.

She swatted my leg playfully, "Sorry Will, I couldn't help myself. I mostly did it in hopes that it would get Shannon to liven up a bit. We had all gotten into a rut after what happened with you-know-who."

I did my best to fight the flush out of my face and made some noise of understanding. I looked over at her from the corner of my eye. She had closed her eyes again, and I took the chance to really look at her.

Shannon had the type of natural beauty that sucked up all the attention in the room, even if she didn't want to. There was no ignoring her presence when she was around.

Alicia, on the other hand, had the type of beauty you could only come to appreciate if you really took the time to study her features. She had a model's cheeks and jawline, with a neck to match her height. Her lips were pale but still held a prominent shape that would catch everyone's eye if she ever bothered to wear lipstick. And yet, even as I admired her, some small part of me still drifted back to Shannon. I didn't understand it yet; why did the person who barely tolerated me seemed to pull at my thoughts harder than the one smiling next to me?

I was staring at her fully when she opened her eyes again and caught my staring. I looked away as quickly as I could, but there was no denying that I had been gawking openly at her.

"Hey, Will?"

"Y-yeah?"

"You wanna go to my house and practice making out?"

I refused to look at her, not wanting to give in to the same trick twice, "Haha, you're hilarious."

"I'm serious. Have you ever kissed a girl?"

"Yes, I have, actually." I lied.

"Okay, but have you made out with one?"

I didn't say anything, not wanting to admit my inexperience. I finally caved and risked a look at her. She was still laying completely motionless and staring up at me. Her face was carefully blank, as if she didn't want to give away what she was thinking. Her eyes, though, held an earnestness to them that I couldn't miss.

"You are going into high school in less than two months, it'll probably be best to have a chance to try it before you go into the deep end," she said with an oddly soft edge to her voice.

"Are… Are you toying with me or something?"

"No. I don't have a boyfriend or anything, and really don't want one," she confessed. "But I've made out with a handful of boys before."

"Yeah, but, we aren't dating or anything."

"So? We don't have to be dating to make out, dumbass."

The girl that was careful and caring the day before, the one who had cleaned my cut to make sure I was okay and checked over me for problems, seemed to be an entirely different person now. She seemed like a hungry predator that was waiting to pounce. But maybe she was just confident. Maybe that confidence scared me more than I wanted to admit.

When I went home for dinner that evening, I floated upon a cloud of confusion and excitement. She made me promise not to act weird after our 'training session', and I assured her I would be *so normal*. When we started, she told me plainly that I was one of the worst kissers she'd ever met, but by the end she had given me the 'Alicia Crash Course' and was pleased with my progress.

Later, lying in bed, I replayed the afternoon again and again in my head; every nervous glance, shaky breath, and inch of space between us shrinking until it vanished. It was the first time I'd ever felt chosen. Not tolerated. Not pitied. Chosen.

Still, even as I drifted off to sleep with the imagined ghost of her taste still on my lips, I couldn't help but think of another girl's eyes: green, cold, and impossible to read.

And that feeling… It was addicting.

Chapter 6
Three Coins

The next day I met the full Caver Gang in the field. I tried to act as if nothing had happened, but whenever Alicia caught my eye heat flooded my face. She never mentioned it, and the others paid no notice, so we headed into the trees along the same narrow trail of packed leaves and half-buried roots.

This time we followed the creek's current instead of fighting it. Water slipped past in thin ribbons, louder than anyone's voice. Mid-morning sun striped the path, laying bands of gold and shadow across our backs. Allen tossed out a joke once or twice, but the laughter died quickly, swallowed by the hush of the woods.

At a two-lane road we climbed the gravel shoulder. A single pickup rattled past, then silence returned. Fifteen minutes deeper, the forest opened into a clearing of briars and grass up to our knees. No birds here, only the distant rush of water and our own breathing.

Theo slowed and searched the brush as if reading landmarks no one else could see. He led us along a faint deer track until the grass ended at a sudden wall of rock. A narrow cave mouth waited there, less an entrance than a dark split in the earth. No one spoke. Allen hefted his stick, then set it down. Shannon's jaw locked. Alicia's small sigh barely stirred the air.

To the left of the entrance stood a limestone slab. Not as large as The Rock, yet solid enough to feel permanent. Lichen covered the lower half, but the upper third had been scrubbed clean. Deep-cut letters, filled with bronze, caught the light in flashes of brown gold.

I stepped closer. The metal lines were warm in the sun while the stone stayed cold. A faint smell of pennies after rain lingered around it.

The inscription read:

THREE COINS FROM YOUR POCKET WILL BUY YOU AN ANSWER:

ONE COIN FREELY GIFTED, ONE MADE IN A BARGAIN, AND ONE WRONGLY LIFTED.

I read it twice before turning to Theo and Allen, who were picking up sticks from the ground and studying them, two botanists discovering new species. "What does this mean?"

Allen refused to meet my eyes while Theo seemed to struggle for words. Finally, Shannon cut in and pointed toward the mouth of the cave. "I think it's probably best if you go in and find out for yourself."

I thought about protesting, but decided against it. Instead, I squared up with the cave as I had done with Beginner's Maw and started to step forward. Allen caught my hand before I could and said softly, "You need to leave your watch and bag out here."

"What? Why do I need to leave my watch?"

Theo nodded aggressively. "Good catch man. Yeah, no electronics or light sources are allowed in with The Oracle."

I looked between the two, thinking it was some kind of joke, but when neither budged I relented and left my watch and backpack with them.

I moved into the mouth of the cave and was immediately greeted with the feeling of air pushing from my back into the depths of the cave. It wasn't a breeze so much as a long, deliberate inhale, as though the cave had lungs and I had already wandered too near their edge. Unlike Beginner's Maw, there was almost an immediate hook after the entrance, eliminating any light much sooner than my previous experience. Behind that bend the dark felt viscous, a living pitch that clung to skin and stripped sound from my ears.

The traversing was much easier, though, and I was able to slowly walk forward in the dark, one hand on the ceiling while the other blindly groped before me for anything I might smack into otherwise. Even so, every step landed an inch deeper than expected, as if the floor kept flexing downward to coax me farther from escape. I reached a wall and felt carefully along it and found another bend that led further down without the ceiling drooping more. Cold beads of condensation slid over my knuckles, but the stone itself stayed warm, flesh that had turned to rock but forgotten how to die.

As I inched forward, I heard a faint skittering sound coming from much deeper inside the cave. A single scrape at first, needle-fine, then another—multiplying, echoing, braiding together until the dark seemed full of brittle legs. My body reflexively froze in place and my breath seized in my throat. That breath felt stolen, not held, the air itself reluctant to return what it had taken. I stood there without breathing for what felt like minutes, listening for any more of the distant, alien sound. Soon the thud of my heart in my ear took away any chance of hearing the faint sound again. It pulsed like a drum summoning something older than language.

I reassured myself, once more, that if the others had done it before, then the descent deeper into the cave couldn't be as dangerous as my mind was making it out to be. **Yet even that thought arrived muffled, stripped of weight, the dark grinding it down before it fully formed.** I let out the deep breath I had been holding tightly in my chest and continued my slow creep deep into the darkness. The length of this portion seemed about half as long as the previous before it also cut hard back on itself. The air behind me collapsed with a dull pop, sealing the corridor the way water seals around a sinking stone.

I had taken five steps past the latest bend when I felt a hot breath across the back of my neck. It carried the stink of minerals and rot—age made gaseous. I flinched hard and lashed at the empty air behind me. The insectile sound was suddenly all around me, a cacophony of a thousand knife blades chipping against the stone walls. Every strike felt aimed at marrow, not muscle, wanting something hidden deeper than bone.

It's often said that you find out what kind of person you really are when faced with life threatening damage. I'm proud to say that I stood my ground and did my best to pinpoint the source of the loud rushing sound, pulling my fist to block my face the way my father had drilled into me after a brutal stint of sixth-grade bullying.

So, when I felt the next burst of hot air on my right cheek I immediately threw my left fist in that direction as hard as I could. I met with thin air and was rewarded with the most sickening sound of laughter I could ever imagine. It wasn't one voice but several, layered: a child's giggle dragged across rusted wire, an old woman's rattle, a beast's throaty hiss, each riding the other until I couldn't tell where one ended.

Before I could retract my fist away, I felt something wrapping itself around my extended arm. It had thousands of cold, dull limbs that propelled it in its path to spiral over my limb, an unimaginably huge centipede made of cold metal. I fought against whatever had enclosed my arm, but couldn't pull away from it, a shrill scream escaping my throat. Rather it would have if whatever had bound my arm hadn't already wrapped itself around my mouth to prevent the call for help.

The horrendous laughter continued, right next to my right ear, only stopping once it was cut off by a wheezing cough. Through the cough, the terror that had bound me spoke, its voice so quiet that the cave's walls didn't even allow it to echo.

"A fighter the Cavers have sent this time," the thing whispered in a voice made of grit and strained vocal cords. Then the voice changed, lilting and feminine. "So rare is the one that would dare strike out at me."

I tried to thrash my way free of its grasp, but the creature held me tightly in place. I couldn't even open my mouth to bite at the appendage that kept my mouth closed.

"No coins in your pockets, little wolf," it crooned, now in the voice of a teenage boy. A voice I didn't recognize, and yet felt carved from the same strange alloy of sweetness and violence that I carried inside my own ribs. "Soooo, no answers. But I'll give you something else. A truth, maybe."

Her grip constricted just enough to make me feel it wasn't a suggestion. Then came her real voice, close and slick and full of scale. Dry and hissing. The voice of something that lived under stone and never blinked. "You play at being a hyena, yet you wear the wolf's skin well, little one. Never forget who you really are!"

I tried to jerk my arm away, but her grip tightened again, this time with something sharper in the embrace. It wasn't crushing. Just a reminder that it could be.

"When you come back," she murmured, now in Alicia's voice, impossibly soft, "and you will come back, bring me three coins. And don't waste my time with coward's questions. Bring me the one that would hurt the most to answer."

Then, without warning, she was gone. No slow release. No slither of departure. Just a whip-crack absence. The skittering sound receded, not into the distance but into the walls themselves.

I was alone.

Panting. Shaking. My skin slick with fear and sweat. I couldn't see anything, but I could still feel the lingering outline of her hand on my face, like a sunburn that hadn't faded.

It would be years before I understood the weight of what she had called me. Even longer before I realized a wolf doesn't ask questions. It stalks, devours, and then buries the bones.

I should have turned back then.

But of course, I didn't.

Chapter 7
Held Breath

I slowly released the breath I held so tightly, letting out a stuttering curse. I groped at the darkness around me until I found a wall to slide down, holding my face in trembling hands. I tried my best to come to grips with what had just happened– to imagine what had held me in place and whispered in such a foul variety of voices.

Eventually, it hit me: The Oracle wasn't the cave at all. It was a creature living inside it – something old and alive that I had just met in the dark. I don't know how long I sat there in the silence, hands shaking, my mind scrambling to convince itself that I hadn't completely lost touch with reality. It felt like I had stepped out of the world and into a myth, and I couldn't tell which parts of me I'd get back.

Once I felt like my feet could support me, I stood and began my stumbling way back to the entrance. Unlike Beginner's Maw, the return trip was no easier than the entering, even with the additional space that made movement 'easier'. I kept moving though and soon I was greeted with the graying of the darkness, finally able to see my hand moving in front of my face, I did my best to collect myself into a semblance of bravery. I marched forward into the light of day once more, finding the Cavers all sitting near the mouth of the cave with varying levels of anxiety plastered over their faces.

Allen was the first to notice me, his look of worry instantly washed away and replaced with his foolhardy smile. He stood but made no movement to approach, instead crossing his arms like a proud father.

After he stood, though, it woke the others from their quiet contemplations, each quickly turning to face me with varying degrees of relief showing past their features.

Alicia was the only one to rush forward to check my exposed skin for injuries. If Allen looked like a proud father, she acted as an anxious mother. "What did it say? Did it hurt you, Will?"

"I'm okay, I'm okay," I protested, though it didn't stop her from lifting my shirt to check my chest for hidden pains. I told them of the brief encounter, and they all nodded as if they expected no less. "What was it?"

"Who knows," Shannon offered with an indifferent shrug. Something about her stance and studying glare put me on edge. "All of us have spoken to it, but no one has ever seen it."

"Electronics don't work in that cave, for some reason," Theo elaborated as he wrapped an arm around my shoulder. "Any fire you carry in with you goes out after the first bend, and lighters won't light. Whatever The Oracle is, it doesn't want to be seen."

"What about the coins? Have any of you-" I suddenly felt ashamed for asking. The question felt like something incredibly private.

"Shannon and I have asked a question," Theo confirmed. The way he worded it confirmed the feeling I had: you didn't ask a Caver their question or for the answer they received.

We milled about for a few minutes before hiking back to the

field. We spent the rest of the afternoon talking and tossing a ball between us. They all avoided asking the one question that hung over our heads: Would I go back to The Oracle? Would I gather the three coins?

Even if they had asked, if I were being honest, I wouldn't know how to answer.

We all decided to meet up at Alicia's house the next day and make plans for the next day and possibly watch a rated-R movie from her dads budding DVD collection. Once everyone split up and headed their separate ways home, I tagged along beside Theo. While the other three lived on the same street as the field, Theo lived on my street near the end of the H's dead end.

"Hey, you asked it a question," I started, offering a defensive hand up toward his immediate reaction. " I just wanted to know if it was worth it."

His face took on a distant expression, before letting out a deep sigh. "I think so, but it's hard to know. Like… you know what djinns are?"

"Genies?"

"No- Well, sorta. You'll probably have Ms. Brown for Freshman English, so you'll learn more about them then, but for now, think of Djinn as Genies that want to fuck you over with your own wish."

I was confused as to what he was getting at, but nodded my understanding anyways.

"I think this Oracle thing might be like that- like it answers your question, but only in a way that ends up hurting you."

"What makes you think that?"

We had reached the intersection next to my house, where he would head left toward his house and I would head into my own driveway. He stood silently, looking up at some clouds that drifted lazily overhead. "I don't know, but I can tell you that what it told me hasn't come true yet, and I don't know how much more time it has left to come true."

Before I could ask anything else he clapped me on the shoulder and started toward his house down the street. I stood there, watching after him until he was nearly in his own yard before heading inside.

That night I lay awake in my bed, the darkness of my basement bedroom feeling more claustrophobic than the depths of Beginner's Maw. Any moment I expected to hear the skittering of The Oracle. When I finally slept, it was a restless night of tossing and turning, though I didn't remember any nightmares the following morning.

Chapter 8
How to Kiss

Over the next two weeks we met up and had the little adventures that made summer breaks oh so important for young teenagers. We watched a few movies together at Alicia's house, played tag football in the field, explored the lengths of Shit Creek, and I even got to practice making out with Alicia one of the days that everyone else was taken up.

Those times I was alone with her, she was a totally different person. When the Cavers gathered, she was the worrying motherly figure that made sure everyone was fed and safe. When we were alone, she was an eager, hands on sculptor that wanted to mold me into her ideal play thing.

It was during one of these teaching sessions that I spotted the black dots just above her right breast. They matched the ones on Shannon and Theo's shoulders perfectly. I had made up a theory in the back of my mind after learning that those two were the only ones that had asked questions of The Oracle. Alicia having the same marking gave me pause, and I pulled away from her, staring at the spots.

"Shit," she mumbled once she realized I had seen the marks, pulling up her tank top more to cover the blemishes.

"Wait, what are those?" I asked, raising a brow.

"They're nothing," she said, pulling away and shattering the intimacy of the previous moment.

"They're something," I protested as I adjusted myself to be more comfortable. "I saw them on Shannon and Theo's shoulders."

"Listen, Will," Alicia said as she pulled her long legs up under her more, "You can't tell the others. Please."

"I won't, but you need to tell me what they are first."

"Yeah, fine."

My theory was right, it turned out. If you brought The Oracle three coins and asked it a question, you were marked with the two dots after you got an answer. She had gone in secret to The Oracle and asked it a question, and she had been upset with the answer, so she never told the others that she had done it.

After a long pause I let out a sigh, "Is it against the rules to ask what your question was?"

She looked away and shook her head ever so slightly, "It's not, but it's just… not done."

I couldn't put my feelings for Alicia into words, but I could tell she didn't want me to ask.

So, I didn't.

If I had known then what I know now, I would've asked without hesitation. It would've stopped me from making the series of choices that led me here, telling this story.

The mood was sufficiently dead, so the two of us decided to throw a movie on and just relax for the rest of the afternoon. We were halfway through American Pie when we fell back into making out. It was twenty minutes after that there came the unmistakable hard knock of Allen on her front door.

I did my best to straighten my clothes and get into a position that looked innocent. She adjusted her own attire and went to the door, opening it with a casual nod to Allen and Shannon.

"Hey, Will's mom said he was here?" Allen said, peering past her shoulder into the living room, where I gave a wave from the sectional. "Oh sweet, he is here. What were you two up to?"

Alicia had moved out of the way to wave them in, "Watching American Pie again. I think Will just likes to see the titties."

I gave out a weak protest as Allen plopped down next to me, rewinding a bit the previous scene. Shannon had taken a couple steps in, but her eyes seemed to dart over Alicia and then me in an analytical way. It was like we were an open book and she had no trouble reading the situation.

"I thought you two were going to go see your dad today?" Alicia said as she took up a spot on the opposite portion of the sectional as if she had been there the whole time.

"We were with him, but he got called in as support for a big fire. Were you two not expecting guests?" Shannon asked, a judgmental edge to her tone.

"It's fine, the movie was getting boring and we were thinking about going out to ride bikes."

"Awww, but this is my favorite part," Allen whined. He gave an exaggerated sigh but hopped up quickly anyways. "All right, what do we wanna do?"

"We can get a football game going," Shannon said, the beginning of a wicked grin creeping onto her lips.

"That sounds good. Me and Will can gather kids on his street and you two can get the kids on this street. We will meet you two in the field," Allen offered.

The two of us set out, and once we were half way up the connecting street he looked over his shoulder back toward Alicia's house. He gave my shoulder a playful punch and chuckled under his breath, "Will, you sly dog you."

"Wh- What do you mean?" I asked as he rubbed at the spot he had tapped.

"Oh, don't play dumb. You and Alicia? Really?"

"It's not like that!"

"Is it not? Because it definitely looked that way when we showed up. I've never seen your cheeks that red."

"It's… It's complicated. We aren't dating or anything."

"Ooooh," Allen said with a nod, "It's one of those situations."

"What do you mean 'one of those situations'?"

"I mean," Allen said with an unsure motion of his hand.

"She just wanted to teach me how to kiss, that's all!"

"Oh, that's all? Kinda like she did with Theo."

My face snapped to stare at him involuntarily, an immediate jealousy exploding in my chest. But his look told me everything. He had caught me in a trap. "You're an asshole."

"And you are a horny fool. I'm sorry dude, but you're gonna get your heart broken."

"Why do you say that?"

"Because she isn't into you," he said, just as easy as breathing.

"What? Why do you say that?"

Allen's face was unreadable for a moment before he threw a glance over to me, "Because I can tell, man. I'm sorry."

I couldn't think of anything to say, so the two of us walked for a couple of houses without speaking. A thought bubbled to the surface of my mind and I broke the silence with a hushed tone, "Why haven't you asked The Oracle anything?"

Allen seemed taken aback by the sudden question, but rolled with it anyway, "I can't think of a question worth asking."

The two of us joked about silly questions until we reached the first house. After we gathered a few kids we returned to the field and played until it was time for everyone to return home. Shannon didn't miss a single opportunity to 'tag' me into the dirt again. It felt more aggressive than before, like she was angry with the conclusion she had come to about mine and Alicia's time alone.

I went home that evening with a couple of grass stains and bruised knees, though I didn't complain. Some part of me felt like she had every right to be angry with me, even though that made no sense.

Chapter 9
Pelts

For the week after my conversation with Allen, I did my best to forget about The Oracle.

And I failed horribly.

The two weeks after my encounter had small moments of consideration for the creature, but for the most part my hormone drenched mind was preoccupied with the confusing feelings I was developing simultaneously for Alicia and Shannon; though, if I'm being completely honest, it was more about figuring out the next time I could meet up with Alicia alone.

This week, in contrast, my mind was plagued by what question I would ask.

Doing dishes after lunch: How do I become the richest man ever? You can't.

Folding my laundry: Is there life outside of Earth? Yes, but you'll never prove it and everyone will think you are crazy if you try to convince them.

Watching 'Scary Movie' with the Cavers: How do I help the most people? Offer yourself up as an organ donor.

Every question I could think of led me into a depressing answer from the back of my mind. If Theo was right, and The Oracle never gave straightforward answers, what was the point of worrying about it?

Watching Allen play Grand Theft Auto 3: What is the

meaning of life? There isn't one.

Eating dinner with my parents: When do I meet my soulmate? You don't have one.

Riding my bike around the neighborhood: What will truly make me happy? You never will be.

It was one of the rare nights that my mom let me go out after dinner, pedaling about the dusk cloaked streets with Allen and Theo, that I came up with the question I wanted to ask: When and how do I die?

To my teenage self, this was such a simple question and obvious question. If The Oracle told nothing but the truth, that meant I would be able to easily plan the rest of my life and be truly free to pursue whatever I wanted, knowing that my fate was already set.

I didn't share the epiphany with the two of them, keeping the lightbulb moment to myself. Maybe if I would've ran the question past one of them, they could've stopped me from asking that question.

I know now– better than anyone else on this planet– the harm such a question can lead to. That question led me to every terrible decision I made going forward.

That night I dreamt of an old woman at the mouth of a cave, her back to me. She was hanging animal skins at the entrance: racoons, deer, squirrels, among many others. To my shock, each of the animal pelts possessed the face of a human ranging in age from teenager to elderly. Once she had finished, she turned and faced me. Two sapling trees sprouted from the bloody, empty pits where her eyes should have been. She pointed a crooked finger back at the last five pelts she had hung up. I realize, in horror, that these had the faces of the Cavers: Theo a bear cub; Allen a fox; Alicia a massive rabbit; Shannon a white-tailed deer; and, finally, my own face frozen in terror atop a grey wolf pelt.

I woke up with a start, confused by the nightmare and its meaning. I went about my morning with the lingering image in the back of my mind. I did my best to distract myself from it, hyping myself up about the fact I was going over to Alicia's this morning. I took a long shower and ate leftover pizza from dinner the night before. Everyone was busy until past three o'clock, and the two of us were going to get in more 'practice' until we met up in the field.

I knocked on her door and stepped back, looking around absently as not to be staring at her when she opened the door. I must have woken her up, since she answered the door in a baggy tee and with the worst state of bedhead I could imagine.

She guided me to her room– a big departure from our normal spot on the sectional in her living room. She directed me to sit on the bed while she went to the bathroom across the hallway to straighten up. Sitting there on her bed, listening to the brush work its way through her hair, I began to spiral around what the change in venue could mean. My breathing picked up and my eyes darted around the room, looking for any other signs that she had planned something different for the day's activities. The sound of her shower kicking on sent me even deeper into the spiral, on the verge of hyperventilating.

The bathroom door cracked open and she stuck her head out– a bare shoulder also lingering in view– and said, "Shit, sorry Will, you can throw something on the TV if you want, I'll be a minute."

"I'll wait here, no worries," I stammered, worried that if I moved from the bed that I might never be invited back to it.

She gave a nonchalant shrug and shut the door, leaving me to my overactive imagination. I imagined her naked form showering in the next room over and did my best to adjust myself in a way to hide my excitement, when a thought came to me.

Looking back at that moment now, I'm embarrassed that this thought entered my mind. It's not something I'm happy with, but I will admit to it. I do so since I think it is crucial in showing the state of mind and the confused feelings I was suffering from.

Sitting there, thinking that I was about to lose my virginity, the thought that forced itself into the forefront of my mind was *Will Shannon ever fall for me if I lose my virginity to Alicia?*

I have no excuse for this, and I know my consideration should've been for Alicia, but that was what I was worried about at that moment. I had some sliver of self-awareness though, and immediately felt guilty about the thought. I decided that if Alicia wanted to go that far with me, I was willing to go with her.

Alicia got out of the shower, again wearing her baggy nightshirt, and said that her period was kicking her ass. She just wanted to lay on the couch and watch a movie and said I could head home if I wanted to. I told her that it was alright and stayed with her. We watched some Rom-Com, her head laid in my lap while I ran my fingers through her curly mess of hair.

I remember her laughing at some corny line the male lead made, and as I looked down at her she looked up at me with the most genuine smile I could imagine.

When I think of Alicia now, that is the moment I think back to. That smile.

She's right to hate me now.

Chapter 10
Gifted. Bargained. Lifted.

The short poem at the entrance to The Oracle's cave spelled out guidelines for the three coins I would need to gather.

One had to be a gift. That would be easy enough; I just had to ask Mom for a quarter and let her 'gift' it to me. I only hoped that asking her for it wouldn't remove the gift quality from the coin.

The second had to come from a 'bargain.' I took that to mean I needed to sell something. Luckily, one of the twins was obsessed with Pokémon cards, and I had some rares I didn't really need, so I figured I could trade a card for a quarter. Fair deal.

The third needed to be stolen, which gave me pause. I wasn't about to shoplift or anything huge. It would be simple enough to swipe a coin from the car's cupholder the next time I was out with Mom, but would that count? It felt thin, but it was the most I was willing to do.

That Saturday, I put my plan into action. After breakfast, Mom was heading out shopping, and I volunteered to go with her. At Walmart, I asked for a dollar for a soda; she gave me two, telling me to grab drinks for both of us. They were seventy-five cents each, so I pocketed two quarters and rejoined her.

She didn't ask for the change. That counted as a gift, right?

We spent the next hour and a half grocery shopping. On the way home, Mom stopped at her usual gas station to fill up. While she went inside to pre-pay, I pulled one of the two 'gifted' quarters from my pocket and dropped it into the loose-change cup. Carefully, I fished out a different quarter from the cup—one she'd earned as change from some earlier purchase—and slipped it into my other pocket, making sure I didn't mix them up. My heart pounded from the small theft, barely a crime at all, but it would have to do. I didn't know if that horrible creature cared about which coin was which, and I didn't want to risk losing my chance.

Once we got home, I helped Mom unload the groceries. When we finished, I told her I needed to run over to the twins' house before lunch. I dropped off my two quarters in my dresser drawer, keeping them separated so I could remember their origins clearly. Then I grabbed my binder with the rare Pokémon cards I'd amassed during my brief collecting phase.

Kelly—the girl half of the fraternal twins—wanted two cards for two quarters, while her brother wanted one card for another quarter. They were definitely getting the better deal, but I didn't care. I made the trade, pocketed the last quarter, and rushed home for lunch.

Gifted. Bargained. Lifted.

With my three coins collected, all I needed now was a chance to visit The Oracle's cave without the other Cavers noticing or tagging along.

Chapter 11
Untouched Section of Limestone

I found my chance two days later. It was the last Monday of July, and my mom's first day at her new job at one of the factories in the city, six exits down the interstate. She packed lunch and left it in the fridge with a note: Be home by five. Don't make me worry.

Allen and Shannon were spending the day with their dad. Theo was still at football camp for the week. Alicia texted to say she felt awful, curled up with a heating pad and wanting to die.

It was the perfect opening.

No one would notice I was gone.

I packed my backpack slowly, like the act might talk me out of it. Sandwich. Chips. Three bottles of water. A notebook. A pen. I clipped my watch to the hand-loop on top, away from my wrist. I didn't want to forget and carry it into the cave by accident.

Each coin went into a different pocket.

Gift.

Bargain.

Theft.

I whispered each word as I slipped the coin into place, sealing each pocket like a ritual. I didn't know if it was reverence or fear, but separating them felt right. Like naming them meant I could still control what they were.

The field was empty. I crossed it without looking back and slipped into the woods. The path to Shit Creek was familiar, but quieter now. More alert. The trees leaned in. Light fractured across the undergrowth. Every snapped twig made me flinch, like the forest already knew how this would end.

I kept walking.

Eventually, the clearing opened like a breath I didn't know I'd been holding. The stone stood just past the trees: weathered, ancient, and half-swallowed by moss.

Still waiting.

I sat down and set my backpack beside me. I ate slowly, without tasting anything, just listening to the trees. The wind. A bird overhead. I finished one bottle of water, then walked to the edge of the clearing to piss.

When I returned, I stood in front of the stone. The bronze inlay caught the light and scattered gold-flecked patterns across the dirt. I ran my fingers over the carved letters, mouthing the words like a prayer I didn't understand.

THREE COINS FROM YOUR POCKET
WILL BUY YOU AN ANSWER:

ONE COIN FREELY GIFTED,
ONE MADE IN A BARGAIN,
AND ONE WRONGLY LIFTED.

I wondered who had written it. Who had taken the time to

etch something sacred into stone and fill it with metal. I reached for the blank space beneath the lines, feeling the smooth, untouched section of limestone. Was it a placeholder? A warning? A name that had never been carved?

I pressed my palm to it. Not to open anything. Just to feel it. Just to see if it felt different today. It didn't. After a while, I let my hand fall.

Then I looked to the cave, not finding any excuses to prolong any more.

Not Beginner's Maw. Not a game. Not some handshake initiation with grins at the end.

This was The Oracle.

I'd been inside before. I'd felt what lived there.

And now, I was going back. Alone.

I took one last breath and stepped forward, into the dark that would shape the rest of my life.

Chapter 12
At Twenty-Three

It was just past eleven a.m. when I stepped into the darkness of the cave. I reached the first bend and headed into the deeper darkness that awaited me. I traversed the first section much faster than before, my left-hand keeping contact with the wall instead of the ceiling. I reached the second twist with far less anxiety and even a flicker of excitement.

As I moved through the second section, groping at the darkness with my right hand, I had a creeping sensation that something was different. Despite moving faster, it felt like reaching the third bend took longer than it should have. I chalked it up to nerves and continued on.

I reached the next turn much faster than expected, but what I noticed first was that the bend went the wrong way. The cave had zig-zagged like a lightning bolt before: one right, one left, repeating. I had just made two rights in a row.

Panic bloomed in my chest. Maybe I had spaced out and taken a left without realizing. That had to be it. I moved on more slowly, my focus razor sharp. This section again dragged on until finally I reached another right turn.

I kept pushing on, refusing to believe I'd come to a third right. The dark pressed closer. The wall grew slick beneath my palm; the stone was sweating from within, not damp with the air's moisture. The rock was too warm for that. It felt fever-hot and too *alive* for comfort.

Soon my footsteps stopped echoing. At first, I thought it was a trick of the acoustics. Maybe the tunnel had curved again. The floor still felt solid under my shoes.

But then I realized I couldn't hear my own breathing. I whispered a curse, just to test my voice. Nothing. The cave swallowed all sound.

My hand brushed something. Not stone. Something soft.

I pulled back by instinct but knew I couldn't keep going without the wall. Slowly, I reached out again.

Just stone. Normal. Cold.

I kept walking.

The passage narrowed. The air turned humid, edged with sourness. Every few feet, the temperature changed. Cold. Then warm. Then cold again.

I lost count of the turns. Some were shallow. Some weren't even turns at all.

At one point I was sure I'd looped back. Another moment, I thought I'd gone too deep, like I'd step through the floor and drop into fire.

I reached up to touch the ceiling. Cold emptiness.

It had never been out of reach before.

No one knew I was here. How long would it take before they even noticed? Could I survive long enough to be found?

My spiral was interrupted by a faint skittering sound deeper in the cave. I focused. I had a goal. I could worry about escaping after. I clenched my jaw and moved toward the sound. The wall stretched on for what felt like yards. Before, each section was shortened. Now the cave refused its own blueprints.

Another bend. Another right. A few steps forward, then the thunder of clattering limbs echoed from all directions. I braced for the claws, but this time it was a cold, leathery hand that grabbed my right wrist and yanked me sideways. It let go. I lost the wall. I was stranded in darkness with nothing solid but the floor.

I grounded my heels and took a defensive stance. Panic and flailing would get me hurt. The unsettling noise intensified, masking its source. And then The Oracle was on me; millipede legs moved over my body in waves, clinging to fabric, catching skin. They gripped—not to pinch and gouge, but to explore. To taste. To savor.

In my left ear the high-pitched babble of an infant, gurgling laughter twisted into something reptilian and wrong.

In my right was a husky, almost tender voice. "The fighter returns. Still breathing. Still bleeding. Still brave enough to face us."

"I brought your coins," I said with a bravery that wasn't even remotely real.

The limbs vanished. In their place: dozens of warm, gentle hands. They touched like worshippers. Or lovers. Or surgeons. They explored every inch of my body and clothing, nearly lifting me from the cave's floor.

A voice coiled into my right ear like the whispers of every woman I would ever love. Soft, feminine, saccharine. "He brings his offerings. Yes, yes, yesssss. Three little deaths, warm in his pockets. Let us see which one sings loudest."

Then a hiss in my left ear, wet, ragged. The hands along the left side of my body became scales, gliding up under my shirt. One claw tapped my belly, then rested like a knife waiting for permission to violate my innards.

"Speak," rasped a crone's voice, hollow and dry. "Speak, wolf cub. Ask what you came to ask."

Then, without pause, it twisted into the gravelly baritone of Alicia's father: blunt, unquestioning, final. "Ask your question. I will answer it truer than you'd truly want."

I fought back the feeling that I was giving a monster exactly what it needed to hurt me and swallowed hard. "What is the reason for my death, and when will it happen?"

The laughter that followed was wrong in every direction. A mother's chuckle. A hyena's shriek. A priest's broken sob. All layered. All perversely delighted.

Fingertips brushed my cheek. A child's hand. Then a lover's. Then something that was old and withered with too many years to remain human.

A new voice sang out, playful and venomous. That of a scorned lover, attempting to hurt you in the way only they could. "He brings THREE coins, makes TWO questions, and begs for ONE answer!" Each number felt like a stab at my very core.

Then nothing.

Silence fell, a suffocating curtain.

Then Theo's voice emerged from the dark, slow and measured, the sound of a countdown before execution.

"Three." A pause.

"Two." Softer still.

"One." Barely a breath.

"Just as the light will leave your eyes on the night you turn twenty-three." Shannon's voice, sweetened mockery, sharp as broken glass. "Your eyes won't even see it coming. Your skull will split beneath the wheel, and what's left of you will soak the gravel."

A hand, slow and silken, slid beneath my shirt along the right side, caressing me as an over eager lover might. Then Alicia's voice, not hers exactly, but the sound of her right before sleep. Intimate. Damning. "You won't be mourned, little wolf. Every love you could have had, you'll drive away. You'll choose teeth over tenderness. You'll call it survival. They'll call it proof."

Two points of heat flared on my chest like brands where the loving touch pushed. I flinched but could not move away as I felt The Oracle's mark sear itself much deeper than my skin and muscle.

Still Alicia's voice, but now the whisper she used when she first taught me how to kiss. "Do you hear me, wolf cub? You will die. And no one will care."

I wanted to scream. Instead, I begged, "Can… Can I not change this fate?"

The scrabbling stopped. The hands froze. All warmth drained from the cave.

Then came the voice. Not one I recognized, but one I somehow remembered. Old. Patient. Starved. "There is a path," it said. "There is always a path. But it is not the prey who rewrites the hunt."

A chuckle. Cold and giddy. "Glance upon the stone that guards my mouth. There you will see the trail. And if you take it, if you bleed enough of yourself to be unmade and remade into more and less and then… I will see you again."

And then I was alone.

No voices. No movement. Just stillness.

I didn't move. Couldn't.

The air had lost its weight. But something of her had stayed inside my marked flesh.

And something in me had gone.

Chapter 13
Save Myself

Numbly, I reached out and felt the cave wall beside me. Cool, grainy, solid. Its steadiness told me the tunnel had settled back into the shape I remembered and that daylight waited somewhere ahead if I kept moving.

I didn't.

I stayed in the dark and let the truth I had pried from The Oracle settle on my shoulders, heavier each second. What had I expected—a gentle promise that I would die at eighty, tucked in sheets, children at my bedside? I had walked in and asked a butcher for his schedule.

The cave held its breath. A single drop fell behind me, the sound echoing forever before it died. My heartbeat filled the silence, slow and heavy, the only proof I was still alive.

I lost track of time. The smell of wet stone thickened until I tasted metal on my tongue. My calves shook from standing so long. I understood then that knowing the date of your death is the least useful fact a person can carry.

Move. The order felt distant, but my legs obeyed. A smear of grey peeled open ahead, black easing to charcoal, then to smoke, until the mouth of the cave appeared. Wind brushed my face. Somewhere birds argued over seeds. The world had not noticed.

I bent, shouldered my backpack, and clipped on my watch. It felt absurdly light, as if it no longer measured anything that mattered. One glance back showed only blank darkness, perfectly ordinary, as if no god had lived there at all.

Less than five minutes had passed.

Relief never came. My thoughts floated outside my body while the rest of me walked. Sun dazzled the clearing, and the standing stone waited where it always had. New lines gleamed beneath the old poem, bronze still raw, the letters seeming to breathe in the light:

THREE COINS FROM YOUR POCKET
WILL BUY YOU AN ANSWER:

ONE COIN FREELY GIFTED,
ONE MADE IN A BARGAIN,
AND ONE WRONGLY LIFTED.

BUT FIVE COINS FROM YOUR HEART
CAN CHANGE LIFE'S DIRECTION:

GOLD FROM INNOCENCE MISLAID,
SILVER FROM A FRIEND BETRAYED,
ONE OF IRON FROM AN ENEMY SLAIN,
AND TWO OF COPPER FROM A LOVED ONE'S EYES.

I read over it what must have been more than ten times, trying to come to grips with what it meant. The Oracle had said I could change my grisly fate. Was this the 'path' it had spoken of?

Some part of my numb heart kindled, and I fished through my backpack to write down exactly what The Oracle had said and the new inscription on the rock. Not sure what else to do, I began the hike back home.

As I broke out of the woods into the field, I was met with Alicia laying in the sun, arms crossed under her head. She didn't even open her eyes when I stopped next to her, "Have a nice little hike?"

After asking, she opened her eyes finally. All the color drained from her face and she stood up in a flurry of motion, hands gripping my face, "Oh fuck, Will, you didn't…"

She threw a panicked look around the empty field before dragging me toward her house. She took me into her bathroom and pulled my shirt up over my head. She didn't have to look hard to find the two black dots on my right pec.

She leaned against the counter and put her hand over her mouth, eyes darting around, drafting some complex plan inside her mind. I went to say something, and realized that I'd not spoken since asking my question to The Oracle. I went to say something, but only a small squeak came out.

The sound snapped Alicia out of her thoughts, and she looked at me as if seeing me for the first time. She wrapped her arms around me and hugged me tightly. The sensation made me jerk slightly, but I didn't pull away.

Slowly, I started to break.

And then I shattered into a million pieces in Alicia's arms.

Let me leave it there. Let me pass over the sobbing in her arms. Let me not go into the details of how she comforted me in that– my moment of greatest weakness. Let me not speak on how well she treated me, lest I have to reflect on how I hurt her even more.

Let it be said that as I cried in her arms, I began to plan on how I was going to gather the five coins to save myself.

What Three Coins Bought Me:
Shannon

Aiden was some kind of storybook Prince Charming or Greek Adonis. That was, until you got to see through the carefully sculpted facade to the asshole underneath. He made it damn near impossible to see through his bullshit. Any time a crack showed in that perfect persona of his, he'd patch it up before anyone noticed.

I saw through the fakery too late, unfortunately. We had been dating for over five months at the time. We hardly spent any time together to begin with and the sparse time we did spend together at The Rock was filled with his constant pressure to 'take our love to the next level.'

I told him no again. I explained, using far more words than were really needed, that I wasn't interested in sucking his cock if he couldn't even be bothered to try reading my favorite book.

"Whatever," he spat. He pulled away and stood up. "I bet you'd use nothing but teeth anyways. We're done."

The words were expected. What wasn't expected was the sting they brought. I had planned on breaking up with him soon anyways, so why did the sudden rejection hurt?

"And I bet you'd bust before it even got to my lips," I countered.

"Fuck you," he sneered, the words passing over the same lips that had whispered 'I love you' scantily an hour ago.

I knew he didn't. I knew he never had. Even though I knew

those flower words were lies, I wanted to believe them.

Aiden was a vain, self-centered son of a bitch, but I'd stupidly thought I could **fix** him. I even had this stupid fantasy that he'd roll up in his family's Land Rover one day and whisk me out of this dead-end town. I should've known better. People warned me what he was like when he was on the hunt. Aiden was a patient hunter, and I was just another trophy to mount in his case of conquests. I guess this prey was too hard to catch, and bruising his ego one too many times meant he was done. So, he called off the hunt.

When he stormed off it left me at The Rock in the last moments of dusk. I considered crying, decided that was fucking dumb, and decided to instead do my favorite activity at The Rock: Life Guessing.

In the fading light, I lay on my back at the top of The Rock. My finger would find a name at random; I'd trace it with my finger until I puzzled out the letters and their year. I would then imagine myself in their shoes as they carved their name, and the life they had lived since joining the Cavers.

CAROL 7&

I rubbed the last digit over and over. *78? 75? 76?*

It didn't matter.

I was Carol, my permed-up hair perfectly sculpted until I had to crawl through Beginner's Maw. I went home after carving my name, and my parents were happily married. I stole a joint from my older brother's stash, and my friends sat in a tight circle in the night air, passing the weak weed back and forth as we bitched about how unfair the last Football game had been called and that the other team kept fouling Tony. I'd suck Tony's dick once the others left to make him feel better. And he'd love me. And he'd take me—

Shannon was fucking crying. Shannon shouldn't be crying over some dumbass. Shannon was better than that. Shannon didn't need to suck some asshole's dick to feel loved.

Maybe Carol would've, but not Shannon.

I scrubbed the tears off my face and realized how late it was. I'd lost track of time living Carol's life.

I headed home and crawled in through the basement window that Allen always left unlocked for me. I dropped onto the old couch next to him. He was glued to some stupid video game where you steal cars and fight gang members, the one he and Theo loved so much.

"Date with Aiden took a while," he stated in a careful tone.

"We broke up," I said flatly.

Allen said nothing, just playing his game with a purposefully emotionless face. He had warned me, but he would never rub it in my dumb face. Allen was too good of a brother to do that. He also knew I didn't want to talk about it, so he left it alone.

Allen was the best brother a girl could ever want.

I caught a strong whiff of weed. "Charlie here?" I asked.

"Nah," Allen sighed. "He left already."

"You think Helen will stop bringing him around soon?"

"*Mom's* trying her best to keep him away when we're home."

Helen is technically our mom, but after she cheated on Dad

and blew up our family, I refused to call her Mom again. Dad kept insisting that whatever happened between them didn't mean she didn't love me.

Sure, Dad, whatever you say.

"Is that before or after she fucks him instead of Dad?" I asked.

Allen didn't answer, focusing harder on the game to avoid the conversation. No point picking that fight again. We'd worn it out weeks ago.

After a few minutes of silence, I leaned over and rested my head against Allen's shoulder. He tilted his head to touch mine, not even pausing his stupid game.

"I love you, dried up jerk stain."

"I love you, skunk-butted bitch."

I got up and went to my room. I fell asleep furious at the whole damn world—and dreamed I was a deer running free in the woods. By second period on Monday, I caught the first whiff of the shitstorm Aiden had unleashed.

"So, were they all at once, or did they wait turns?" Jessica B drawled, snapping her gum.

I didn't even glance up from my notebook. "Your leg warmers are dumb and you're not making any sense," I said, deadpan.

B ignored me and turned to her friend, Jessica L. "I bet she asked them to do it one at a time," B said loudly. "So, she could enjoy it longer. Slut."

"I bet she even saved some to taste after," L added, making a grotesque little gesture. They cackled and strutted off.

My ears rang and my face burned. Under my breath I

whispered, "Fuck you, Aiden."

The rest of the day was whispers and pointed fingers. I kept my head up and my middle finger (mentally) primed, never letting them see me crack. It wasn't until between fourth and fifth period that I ducked into a bathroom stall and let myself cry.

On the bus ride home, I told Allen about the rumors. His anger went ice-cold and silent. He called Dad.

When I took the phone, I heard Dad's voice, tight with barely-controlled rage. "Hey, Shanana."

That was all it took. I broke. Sobbed. He promised to speak to Aiden's parents.

That night, I lay in the yard staring up at the stars. I needed a real answer, no rumors, no lies, so I made up my mind to go see The Oracle.

By Friday, the bullying was even worse. The obscene *eating* gesture became a routine show in the halls. I kept my chin up and refused to give those assholes the satisfaction of seeing me flinch.

After school I told Allen I was going for a hike.

"I need some air," I lied. He deserved better, but I knew he'd try to stop me.

He eyed me for a long second. We both knew I was full of it, but he didn't push.

"Okay. I love you, cat-turd sandwich," he said quietly.

"I love you, gapped-butt-sniffer."

I headed up the trail to The Oracle's cave. The moment I stepped into the darkness, I heard that familiar skittering in the gloom: fast, rhythmic, everywhere at once.

But this time, she didn't greet me with claws.

Those hands didn't strike; they held. Hundreds of them. Work-worn and eerily familiar. Gentle in a way that was somehow worse than blade-sharp cruelty. A father trying to comfort a daughter after the world has already broken her in half.

I swallowed hard. "I have a question for you," I said into the dark.

No reply. Just the sound of skin against skin, too close, too many. The Oracle, she knew. Of course she knew, she knew the future.

"Will I ever be okay?"

Aiden's voice oozed against my ear, slick and poisonous, like an oil spill on water—shiny on the surface, choking everything beneath. "The wolf strays into the deer's glade."

Theo's voice came next, gentle and clueless. "But the deer… she doesn't run. She watches."

Alicia's voice followed, breathy and afraid. "She thinks if she's still enough, good enough, needed enough… the wolf might stay."

What I imagined was The Oracle's true voice rasped beside my cheek; dry, feminine, and reptilian-slow. "But he is just one fang among many."

Then came a crone's cackle — sugary sweet and mad as hell. "Oh, how the deer seethes when the rabbit takes the wolf instead. She watches them—fuck, and fuck, and fuck—and bites down on her tongue until it bleeds."

A young girl's voice chimed in, too sweet to trust. "She calls the rabbit her friend. Calls her 'little rabbit' when they're alone. But deep in her belly, the deer hopes she chokes."

A teenage boy's voice spoke next, one I didn't recognize—sweet and sharp at once, like a honey-coated blade. "She'll raise her haunches for every hunter that passes: coyote, wolf, lion, jackal. Let them rut. Let them bite. Let them feed. They'll all move on with full bellies, and she'll pretend she liked the taste of her own shame."

And then, curling beneath them all, The Oracle's real voice came again, low and cold: "No, miss deer… you will never be okay. But oh, how well you'll pretend."

...BUT FIVE COINS CAN CHANGE IT.

BUT FIVE COINS FROM YOUR HEART

CAN CHANGE LIFE'S DIRECTION:

GOLD FROM INNOCENCE MISLAID,

SILVER FROM A FRIEND BETRAYED,

ONE OF IRON FROM AN ENEMY SLAIN,

TWO OF COPPER FROM A LOVED ONE'S EYES.

Chapter 14
More Than Halfway to My Deathbed

I told no one of my questions to The Oracle or the damning prophecy it had relayed to me. Alicia knew I had gone to the cave, but much like her, my mark was hidden on my torso and wouldn't be seen by anyone I didn't want to see. As I promised not to tell anyone of her mark, she promised not to tell anyone of mine.

I was a twelve-year-old and I knew I was more than halfway to my death bed. That kind of pressure wasn't meant for such a young mind. It warped every thought I had; changed how I saw things.

As I stood in Alicia's bathroom, overcoming the shakes from my harsh weeping, she ran her hands through my hair and caressed my back with loving tenderness. She cooed and whispered in my ear in hopes to calm my reeling mind. I should have been excited for the closeness and the opportunity to be held by a pretty, older girl.

Instead, I was wondering how to meet the requirements of the 'five coins' that the poem had said would come from my heart.

I don't remember leaving Alicia's house or what I said to her as I left. I remember telling my mom that I was going to lay down and that I didn't want dinner. I remember laying in my messy bed, staring at the ceiling as I turned the words in my mind.

Gold from innocence mislaid.

How did one 'mislay' their innocence, anyway? I couldn't

come to a conclusion for that coin and moved on to the next.

Silver from a friend betrayed.

So, at some point I would have to betray a friend in some meaningful way. Being without friends for so much of my life meant that I treasured the very idea of friends. The Gangers were the best friends I had ever had– even if I had only known them for less than a month. Even so, the thought of betraying any of them made me sick to my stomach. If it meant saving my life, though, maybe I could do it.

One of iron from an enemy slain.

I'd have to kill someone? That seemed impossible. How could I possibly kill someone? That's not the type of person I would ever want to be. And who would I even consider my enemy, anyway? Maybe if someone was so terrible that I considered them my 'enemy' they would deserve to die.

And two of copper from a loved one's eyes.

What the hell did that mean? Did it mean I had to blind someone? No, that didn't make sense. I knew I would have to research what that meant to figure out how hard it would be to get these two coins.

I tossed and turned in bed, trying to get comfortable and failing horribly. Finally, around 10pm, I gave up and climbed from my bed and headed for the kitchen, hoping that grabbing something to eat might help.

My dad was standing with his back to the sink, his hip pushed back against the sink as he ate at a jumbo honey bun. I pulled up short, surprised to see him standing there in his rugged electrician's clothes. Normally I would've noticed the smell of the brewing coffee before I walked up on him, but my mind was far too distracted to even notice it.

"Hey bud, what are you up to?" he asked with a raised brow.

"I skipped dinner, so I wanted to grab a snack before I fell asleep."

He nodded thoughtfully as if I had said something truly deep and moving, "I have truly raised a boy wise beyond his years."

I let out a small chuckle, feeling some part of my built up tension release. "I don't know dad, I've been feeling pretty dumb lately."

"That makes you smarter than any teenager I've ever known."

"What do you mean?"

"Most boys around your age think they know everything, and no amount of proof will sway them."

"Were you like that?"

"Doubly so, yeah." He threw away the wrapper and started to fill his thermos with the fresh coffee. "How have you been enjoying the neighborhood? Mom says you are out of the house every moment she doesn't force you to be inside."

I nodded slightly and leaned against the oven opposite him, "Yeah, I've made some pretty cool friends."

I described each of them and talked about them a little, my dad listening intently as I gushed about how great my friends were. Alicia was the last one I spoke about, and my dad took special interest in her.

"Huh, I should've figured."

"What do you mean?"

My dad let out a mighty sigh and sat his massive hand on my

shoulder, "Listen, you be good to that girl. I can tell by the way you talk about her, she's good to you."

I wanted to protest, but then realized that I had spoken about her for twice as long as anyone else.

"I gotta get to work, bud. I'm off the night after tomorrow, so how about I get up a bit early and we go to that drive-thru down the highway and watch something?"

I smiled. I hadn't gotten to spend hardly any time with my dad since he started his new job as an electrician for the power company, doing dangerous maintenance on the power grid at night. Even though the work was straining and posed a real risk to him, he enjoyed it immensely and it paid well. Unfortunately, it meant he slept all day and worked all night, leaving little time for Mom and me.

He wrapped me in a hug, kissed the top of my head, and tousled my hair. He grabbed up his thermos and went out to his work truck, the dark swallowing him whole before the metallic beast lit up the driveway. As he pulled out of the drive, I waved just in case he could see me. I watched him drive away, munching on one of his honey buns.

Chapter 15
An Oath to Uphold

There were many small things that happened the rest of that summer before school started up. I couldn't focus on much and found little enjoyment in the adventures the Cavers dragged me through. I knew Alicia hadn't told them about my foolish actions, but they could all tell something was wrong with me. To their credit, they all did their best to cheer me up in their own ways.

For that, if nothing else, they deserved better than me.

Nothing helped though.

My first four weeks at Upperpoint High School came and went.

I had found a groove to fit into, and even had a period with Theo and a different one with Shannon. Unfortunately, none of the Cavers from my neighborhood shared my lunch period, so I spent the time at a table with a handful of kids from my classes.

One was a Caver named Steven that Theo introduced me to during our shared P.E. class. He lived in the rich neighborhood that I had heard about from Theo. The one that Aiden lived in.

"I heard you guys had to scratch someone's name from The Rock," I prompted as I poked at my rubbery pizza.

"Oh, Aiden?" Steven shrugged a bit and nodded. "Yeah, dudes an asshole. Jordan said he was breaking the oaths by spreading a rumor about a girl from your group right?"

"Yeah, some pretty bad stuff," I agreed and pushed my tray

away, careful to avoid saying the boy's name. I had an oath to uphold.

"'Pretty bad'? Jesus, underselling much Will?" Jen asked with a dubious gesture. "Aiden said she had a gangbang with five high schoolers when she was in the eighth."

"What's a gangbang?" Joel asked with a confused look at us. He was only 10 but got moved up two grades because he passed some tests.

"It's when a bunch of dudes all get together with one girl and-" Clark started before receiving a sharp elbow from Jen. "Oww! What the fuck Jen?"

"Ask your older brother about it when you get home Joel," Jen said as she threw a dangerous glare toward Clark. "Yeah, Shannon got bullied pretty bad the rest of last year. She seemed to handle it really well though."

My blood was boiling at the mention of what he had really said. It seemed like Jen admired Shannon's ability to handle the verbal abuse she had suffered from her peers.

The next day, during my second period, an unfamiliar teacher rushed into our classroom and whispered something to our teacher. She turned on the monitor in the corner of the room, and my class watched in shock as the second plane hit the World Trade Center.

I don't remember much about the rest of that school day now, but we got sent home early and after talking to my mom for a few minutes, I went over to Alicia's and watched the news on her big screen with the rest of the Cavers. None of us knew what was going on at the time, but the event left us all in a weird mood, and we went our separate ways as our parents got home from work.

I was the last one to leave her house, and before I did, I asked her if she could just hold me for a few minutes.

She obliged the simple request and I held her back, smelling her conditioner as the news in the background went on about their theories of who did the attack. When I pulled away, she looked down and gave me a weak smile.

Looking back on it, I knew she could tell I was hurt, and all she wanted was to fix the pain. Unfortunately, The Oracle had planted the pain so deep that no one was ever going to pull it free.

Chapter 16
Wolf Devouring a Defenseless Rabbit

My birthday was less than a week later. Luckily, for my narrative, most teenagers have a very narrow scope of the seriousness of such world-shaping events. The Saturday before my actual birthday my parents threw a sleepover. The guest roster was an astonishing seven strong, something I never would've imagined in my junior high days. The Cavers were the first to arrive, filtering in in small waves.

My dad was at the bottom of the slope that led into the garage that connected to the basement. He already had the grill going and was making hamburgers and hotdogs to order for the arriving guests. It was his first time meeting them, even though my mom had spoken to all of them at least once.

I watched from the side as some hushed, conspiratorial words from Allen made my dad release a hearted laugh. He gave Allen a lively pat on his shoulder before turning to Shannon.

She had a way with parents, always very polite to them in a way that seemed alien to me at the time. My dad shook her hand gently while she gave a wide, strong smile. She then joined Allen in the living room section of my basement to set up the PS2, sparing me a passing nod and grin. Something seemed off with how happy she seemed for my birthday.

Since my induction into the Cavers she always maintained a distance from me, and spoke to me the least of the group, though I couldn't figure out why. Well, except the time her and Allen had interrupted my 'lessons' with Alicia. Even so, there was something about her that often drew my attention, one of the only things that could distract me from Alicia or the bone-gnawing depression that I now recognize all these years later.

Alicia was the next to arrive, cutting across the yard toward the garage with her backpack casually slung over her shoulder. As she made her way I moved up to meet her at my father, offering to take her bag upstairs for her while she hung out. I heard my dad make a small snicker and I immediately realized that I hadn't made the same offer for Shannon, which only added on to his theory about my feelings for her.

She gave me a warm smile, casting light over some part of me that was held up in shadow. She offered her bag forward as she spoke to my dad about how she'd like her burger. I took the bag and headed into the basement, offering to take Shannon's as well. She gave a shrug and thumbed at the backpack she had dumped off next to the door.

As I came back down the stairs, I met Alicia coming in from the garage. I stopped two steps from the landing and was about to say something when she raised a single finger to her lips. She peered around the corner to make sure Allen and Shannon hadn't noticed her arrival. Once she was sure they hadn't, she stepped up to occupy the step below me to be eye to eye with me. She wrapped her hand behind my head and kissed me suddenly on the stairs.

That kiss was different than every other one we had ever shared, and to this day I can't describe how. It might have been that she was normally taller than me, so being on the same level was a unique dynamic. It could've been the way she was sneaking it in with our friends mere yards away. It might even have been the idea that she would be sleeping under the same roof as me for the first time. Whatever it was, though, it was fleeting and when she broke away she gave me a sly wink before joining the other two, happily greeting them as she called the next round against Allen.

I was frozen there, literally stunned at the brazenness of the moment. Once I had gathered my thoughts I went back out to check if my dad needed anything.

"Nah, I got all the meat I'll need to make everyone's stuff and a couple of beers in the fridge for me," he said as he poked at a burger gently, looking over at me. "You like 'em tall?"

I nearly choked on my own tongue as I looked around, "Wh- Dad, no, it's not like that."

"Will, it's okay. You're turning thirteen in a couple of days, this is to be expected."

I searched for more excuses, but finally gave up and let out a long sigh. "I don't know dad, I... I really like Alicia and we... Yeah, we've made out a few times, sure. But she also made it clear we weren't dating. And... And I'm confused, because I get these feelings around Shannon too..."

My dad listened and slowly nodded in the way he always did when I related a problem to him. My father– for all the faults I would discover as I grew older– truly listened to me and made me feel truly heard. "Courting a girl while you have feelings for another is a good way to end up with coins on your eyes."

The phrase struck me like a lightning bolt. I blinked and tried my best to not show how the phrase had caught me off guard, "Wh- what does that mean? 'End up with coins on your eyes'?"

"Huh? Oh, I figured you'd know about that since you were so into Greek and Roman mythology stuff as a kid. They used to put coins on the eyes of their dead so that they could pay the fee to cross the River

Styx."

I nodded slowly and started walking away, completely forgetting that my dad was trying to help me with my conflicting feelings about Alicia and Shannon. He didn't stop me, probably assuming I had taken to heart what he was trying to convey.

In reality I was lost in the memory of reading the stone outside The Oracle's cave. And two of copper from a loved one's grave, from their eyes. Someone I loved had to die before I could change my fate.

I was in a thoughtful haze when Theo arrived, and he seemed to sense something was wrong. He gave me space and joined the rest of the Cavers on my couch, joking with Allen about one of the teachers they shared in tenth grade classes, but I caught him throwing worried glances in my direction periodically.

I did my best to enjoy the company of my friends, but I couldn't stop wondering if a loved one was going to die before I turned twenty-three. And wondering if I'd be relieved if they did. And if I was relieved… What would that say about me?

We were taking turns playing the fighting game that Allen had rented specifically for the party– Theo handily getting his ass kicked by Shannon– when Steven arrived. He was the first of my lunch friends to arrive and joined us after his parents got done talking to my parents. They were probably checking to see what the plans were for the girls at this sleepover. They were going to be sleeping in the guest room upstairs while the boys all crashed in the basement, to make sure no 'funny business' went on.

I introduced him to everyone, and he recognized Shannon and Theo from our grade, though he had only heard of Allen and Alicia from the Cavers of his neighborhood. Allen played his role as social lubricant perfectly, and soon it was as if Steven had always been part of our Caver Gang.

Shortly after him Jen arrived, and she slotted right in even faster. She wasn't a Caver– yet– and thus was always murky on the details of the group and its rituals of initiation. She lived on the opposite side of the town, really far from Shit Creek. Even so, she was interested, and wanted to join the secretive group.

She also knew that Shannon had been betrayed by Aiden and for that he had been 'struck' from some 'rock'. While she didn't understand the gravity of that situation, she did look up to Shannon for how well she handled it. It can be said that Jen had grown up with less of a filter than most, and so she brought up the subject without thinking anything of it.

"The way you told off the Jessicas in the middle of the lunchroom on the last day of school– it was straight out of one of those movies! You were like the heroine and everything." Jen gushed, doing her best not to stare openly at Shannon.

Shannon gave her a bit of a nod, maintaining a cool demeanor as she looked back at the TV, "Someone had to, those fuckwits deserved worse, honestly."

I watched Shannon carefully, and I saw all the minor expressions that cycled across her forced nonchalance, despite her best effort. I wasn't shocked in the least when she excused herself after the next round and went upstairs to use the bathroom.

I discreetly pulled away from the group and went up the stairs and headed toward the guest bedroom. Across the hall from it was the guest bathroom, but there wasn't any light spilling out from under the door, giving away that it wasn't occupied.

I looked around the corner into the guestroom, seeing Shannon sitting on the edge of the bed, with her face hidden by the cascade of her red hair. Her body made small jerking motions, fighting to keep all of her emotions packed inside her chest.

"H-hey," I offered weakly.

Her face snapped up to stare daggers at me, her eyes puffy and damp with tears, "What?"

I stepped more fully into the bedroom and leaned against the doorway, "I just… I just wanted to apologize for Jen."

"Why? She's fine."

"Then… Why are you crying?"

I felt a wave of dread, like I had said some forbidden phrase.

"It's… Come here, Will."

I blinked in confusion but complied, moving to stand in front of her. She looked up at me and some distant part of me wondered if this was the angle that Alicia saw me from.

"Do you love Alicia?"

The question was a brick colliding with my face.

Did I love Alicia? I had very strong feelings for her, and I couldn't– wouldn't– deny that. But if I loved her, why did I feel like I did in that moment, standing so close to Shannon?

"I… I don't know."

Shannon's cold green eyes had melted away, and they were searching my eyes for something. I don't know if she found it there, but whatever she found there made up her mind for her.

She stood suddenly and kissed me.

And I pulled back. I held her upper arms as I shook my head, trying to grasp what had just happened. By the time I came to my senses, I could see she had found something in that split second of our lips meeting. She pulled away from me and pushed me away with a hand on my chest, "Get down stairs before someone comes looking for you. I'll be down in a few minutes."

Between the all-consuming dread of knowing my fate, the price I would have to pay to change it, and the hormonal roller coaster that was my brain, something broke in me at that moment. What I said next…

It does me no good to dress it up and say more than to simply state what I said in that guest bedroom.

"What the fuck is wrong with you?" She looked as if I had slapped her, but I pressed on. "You throw these looks at me like I'm worse than scum, but sometimes I see these other looks like you want me around, and you act all hateful toward me, but then you kiss me. What the fuck do you want from me, Shannon?"

She reached up and slapped me. It wasn't hard, on the contrary it was quite soft. But it stung all the deeper for its softness. "I want you to leave me the fuck alone and go downstairs." She pointed at the door as if it were her house and I was some nosey intruder. I scoffed and turned around, heading for the door without looking back at her.

The rest of that afternoon went by in a blur. Shannon returned to the rest of us and acted like nothing had happened upstairs. Clark showed up at some point and completed the roster of my friends. Several times Alicia found chances to sneakily kiss on me when she knew no one else would know.

And I kissed her back, hungrily– like a wolf devouring a defenseless rabbit.

That night, laying in the darkness of my basement with all of my giggling male friends, I made up my mind. On my birthday I would ask Alicia out, to be my actual girlfriend.

94

Chapter 17
"Happy Birthday, Will.

As we waited to pile onto the bus on my birthday, I asked Alicia to sit next to me so I could talk to her on the short ride from the school to our stop. She shrugged and gave a small smile. Once we sat down, I let out a deep breath and turned to her, then immediately shut my mouth and looked forward.

"What's up Will? What did you wanna talk about?" she asked with a curious raise of her brow.

I struggled for words for a moment before stammering out, "Is your dad gonna be home?"

She blinked and shook her head slowly.

"Can I come over after I drop off my stuff at home?"

"Yeah, that's fine. Is everything okay?"

I nodded and looked forward, not sure what to say. The constant pressure of my prophecy had lessened a bit. It seemed so far away at that point and I didn't have control over a big part of it anyway, so I had resolved to do my best to enjoy the time I knew I had.

Once the bus dropped us off, I rushed home, dropped off my bag, put on a bit of extra deodorant, and headed over to Alicia's house. When I stepped up to knock on the door, it opened before my knuckles could connect. Alicia stood there with no shirt on, a lacy black training bra catching me by surprise.

"Happy Birthday, Will."

I stuttered and immediately looked around to make sure no one was on the street behind me. She reached forward, and pulled me in to shut the door.

I won't replay that scene beat-by-beat; what matters is that she agreed to be my girlfriend while we laid on her bed and that I didn't 'lose my innocence' that day.

That terrible day was still months away.

Chapter 18
Stone Placed on My Chest

The snow of that February was crisp and harsh in equal measures, adding a new depth to the somber tone of the funeral. As the casket lowered into the waiting grave, Alicia lay a hand across Theo's shoulder. He didn't cry as his mother sank into a hole that she'd never return from; he surely ran out of tears in those final days he spent next to her hospital bed.

But his father hadn't.

Watching a grown man weep that hard made me feel uncomfortable in a way I couldn't articulate, but I stood behind Theo with my hand resting against his shoulder next to Alicia's. Shannon moved around him to hug him tightly while Allen stood back and away, a distant and confused look lingering on his face.

"She… She's not hurting anymore," Theo said with a monotone baritone. I saw Alicia flinch at the words, her eyes tightly shutting against the tears that fought their way out. Shannon made no such effort, crying all the tears that Theo couldn't.

Once the funeral was over, my mom drove me home and the quiet of the car ride pressed a stone to my chest. As we entered the driveway she stopped the car and put it into park. She looked over to me before patting my knee, "Are you okay baby?"

I didn't know how to answer that, so I shrugged. She watched my face for something that wasn't there.

"When you get out of your suit, do you want me to make you something for lunch and then you can go hang out with Alley-cat?"

My mom had taken to calling Alicia Alley-cat after she found out we started dating. She loved her, and was always happy to have her over for dinner if her dad needed to work late.

"Yeah, I think… I think that'd be for the best," I said and suddenly I was crying.

My mom leaned over the center console to hug me as I babbled about how unfair it was that Theo had to lose his mom. She had struggled with her condition for years, and the sudden turn for the worst caught Theo's family off guard. Why did she have to leave her son all alone, and I begged my mom to never leave me alone like that.

After a while I had calmed down and told her I wanted to get changed and to go see Alicia. She pulled into the garage and I quickly went to get changed. Half an hour later I was knocking on Alicia's door. Her dad opened the door and gave me a tired smile, still wearing his button up with a loosened tie.

"Hey Will," he said with a gentle but tired smile.

"Good afternoon sir, mind if I see Alicia?"

He nodded and waved me in, "She's in her room. Keep the door open, okay?"

"Yes sir," I agreed, moving down the short hallway to her room. She was laying on her back, still wearing her black dress, and staring at the ceiling. "Hey, can I come in?"

She looked over at me and gave a forced smile. I joined her on her bed, sitting with my back against her headboard so that she could lay her head in my lap. She had started growing her curly hair out more, and I gently weaved my fingers through it while she hugged my leg.

At some point we fell asleep like that, the intense emotions having drained our energy.

The short nap sent me spiraling into a nightmare.

Theo stood with his back to me, watching as the thousands of insect legs of The Oracle wrapped around Theo's mom and dragged her into a pool of black water. As I watched, Theo reached into the inky pool and pulled out two copper coins. He then turned back toward me and where his eyes should've rested in his head he had two smoldering pits. Slowly he placed the coins over his empty sockets and smiled with a mouthful of blood-soaked teeth.

I woke up with a start, waking Alicia with the sudden motion. She blinked and looked up at me with a questioning look.

"Sorry, just… had a dream."

"Oh. Do you mind stepping out for a second so I can change? Don't think dad would like you in here for it."

"Drats," I said as I stood and headed for the door, earning me a playful slap on the rear. I walked out to the living room and saw her dad sitting on the sectional with a distant look in his eyes. When he raised a brow toward me I thumbed toward Alicia's room, "She's changing."

"Right. Will, have you met Mrs. Daughtry before?"

The sudden question surprised me but I nodded slowly, "Yeah, once. On one of her good days. She really wanted to meet Theo's friends and…" I trailed off, not wanting to mention how badly the meeting had gone. She had been very nice but began vomiting halfway through a sentence. We were excused and Theo apologized profusely for the timing, but we had assured him that we didn't mind.

"I knew her before her condition took such a bad turn," he said with a deep sigh. "Just… Be there for Theo, yeah? I already told Alicia to keep an eye on him too."

I nodded, not sure what to take from the interaction. Alicia poked her head out from her room and I headed back with a pit forming in my stomach.

Chapter 19
Some Fresh Hell

The nightmares picked up in frequency after the funeral. Every night was some fresh hell: Alicia laying in a blood heap as I tore her innards out with clawed hands to consume iron-flavored viscera; Allen slowly driving a dagger into my shoulder while swearing he was a friend and that he'd never hurt me; My father's charred corpse hanging from a powerline, still smoking. All of them held the hoarse laughter of The Oracle as a constant undertone.

I never shared with the Cavers–not even Alicia– how badly my nightmares had become. It felt wrong to broach the topic of my problems while Theo numbly moved through the motions of day to day existence, the life drained from his once friendly face. What did you do to comfort a friend who had lost their mother? I couldn't complain about something so mundane as a loss of sleep and nightmares.

Even so, I think they all could see something was happening to me. I hung out with everyone less and less. I would spend a day or two during the week hanging out with Alicia, and I did my best to make it out to the field on at least one of the two weekend days. My grades slipped overtime and left me struggling to maintain even a C in all of my classes.

The disturbance of my sleep slowly grinded and chipped away at me all the way into the end of May, when it all boiled over. When I started to see things that I shouldn't have.

I was walking through the hallways between classes, in an apathetic daze. Ahead of me, around the corner I was walking toward, I saw a massive centipede's body looping from the corner and back around the blind edge multiple times. The mass of chitin and spindly legs drew a sharp gasp from me, followed by a loud scream. I stumbled backwards, scrambling backwards until I fell, my backpack meeting the tile floor of the hall with a hard thud.

Despite my instincts to keep the threat in my line of sight, I lost it when I fell. When I leaned up in a hurry to find it again– to locate the incomprehensibly massive insect– it was gone. Everyone was staring at me in confusion and I regained my feet asking if anyone else had seen it. No one met my eyes and the murmuring of their confusion drove me forward to find the monstrous form.

Of course, when I reached the corner I was greeted with nothing. Just the stretch of lockers, classroom doors, and students that should be there.

That was only the first of many such hallucinations that began to plague my waking hours. I'd be in math class and see Theo with his head nearly decapitated. I'd be sitting at the lunch table with Steven and Jen when I'd see a wolf with a rabbit hanging from its jaws run through the center of the room. While changing in the locker room for P.E. I had to listen to the sound of The Oracle's thousand legs skittering on the other side of the walls.

The most shocking part was how quickly I became accustomed to the shift in my reality. I can't say that I wouldn't flinch or jump at the sights, but for the most part I could parse the things that didn't belong, and then I'd know they weren't real.

On a Wednesday in early April, I went over to Alicia's as soon as I got off the bus. Her dad was going to be at work until nearly dinner, and mom was pulling a long shift at the factory. I lay on her bed and she straddled me, kissing at me with the hungry passion I had come to expect from her in privacy. I closed my eyes as she began to kiss at my neck and snake her hand toward my crotch. The feeling of her breath against my skin was the first relief I'd found in months, somehow more intense and perfect than any other time.

"Hey, you want a drink?"

I snapped forward and stared in confusion at Alicia standing in the doorway, holding a can of Mt. Dew in an offering way. I felt up to my neck and found something black and sticky there. When I pulled my hand back and looked at it, the black ichor left arching spindles back to my neck. In confusion, I looked back to her, and in the doorway she stood perfectly upright, an invisible force pulling her to her tallest. From her mouth the black ichor dripped like bubbling tar and her eyes held the same copper coins that I had dreamt covering Theo's eyes.

I snapped out of the hallucination by Alicia shaking my shoulders, her voice raised in a panicked alert. I had been screaming in terror myself, I realized, my throat sore with the effort.

She had gone to the bathroom and to grab a snack, I remembered, but in the hallucination she never left. Was the Alicia that sat before me, looking over me for signs that I had hurt myself real?

"I… I think I'm sick, Alley-cat," I admitted. She started to check my head for a fever, her motherly instincts kicking in. "No, no. Like, I think my brain is broken. I've been seeing things and I think I'm seeing the future or a more real reality?"

"Will, what are you talking about?"

I realized that the last part of my sentence made no sense and tried to course-correct. "I've not been sleeping more than an hour a night for almost three months and I think my brain is filling in the gaps."

I could see the puzzle pieces fitting together on her face as she realized all the signs that I had explained away. Then a look of betrayal crept onto her face, "Why didn't you tell me sooner?"

"I'm sorry, I didn't want to worry you, or anyone else."

"Your blood and brains are going to coat the entire dashboard, and your funeral will be a closed casket event," she said in a sympathetic way.

"What?" I said, shaking my head. Nothing I could see made me question the moment, but what she said…

"I said you need to talk to your parents, Will! Maybe they can take you to the doctors and get you some sleeping pills." The worry in her eyes was very real, and I nodded gently, feeling tears forcing their way out of my squinted eyes.

"When you die, I'll have hated you for years and I'll only show up to the funeral to spit on your casket before they lower it," she said, her hands petting me lovingly, comfortingly. I didn't ask her to repeat herself.

Chapter 20
A More Real Reality

Ambien was a blessing and a curse. My parents had me prescribed to help with the sleep disturbances, and it did great at its job. The problem was, it didn't stop the nightmares. Whereas I would kick myself awake within an hour of falling asleep before, now I would experience nightmares without the reprieve of waking myself.

I'd wake from them and feel mentally drained, but my body was rested enough that the hallucinations loosened their grip on my reality. So, it became a balancing game. How long could I go without the Ambien, and how long would I need to be on it before I started to lose my sanity once again.

This balancing act carried me through the summer and soon my fifteenth birthday was sneaking up on me. It was my one-year Anniversary with Alicia and I wanted to do something to celebrate our time together.

In all honesty, I never would've been able to survive the rollercoaster of my existence without her soothing presence in my life. My friendship with the Cavers also grew stronger, especially with Theo. He still struggled with his mom's passing, but was overcoming the burden better than I ever could have. Allen started dating Jen– my lunchroom friend– right before school let out. Her older brother dropped her off to 'hang out with Shannon' at least three times a week throughout most of the summer, and before

June ended we took her to The Rock where she braved Beginner's Maw and carved her name.

Shannon spent less time with the rest of us, but she seemed more even tempered when she was around, though that may have been my sleep-deprived mind not picking up on her snark and snide remarks. The only person she seemed to go out of her way to spend time with was Alicia. If I wasn't with Alicia, Shannon was, and the two started to use each other's mannerisms.

As I entered tenth grade and my birthday arrived, I realized what I wanted to do with Alicia for our one year of dating.

"You can't be serious," my mom said, turning toward me with a surprised look on her face.

"Mom, I swear, I'll be back first thing in the morning," I reassured.

My dad looked between us, having only just caught the last two sentences, "What's going on?"

"Will wants to spend the night of his birthday camping out with his friends in the woods," she said with an edge of disbelief.

My dad looked at me for a long moment and then looked back to my mom, "Let him, he knows those woods better than anyone."

My mom gave him a shocked face. He walked over to her and whispered something in her ear. She blushed and slapped his chest, "You are insufferable!"

I stood awkwardly, not sure I wanted to know what was said. "So…?"

My mom let out a sigh and shrugged, though she shot my dad a sly smile, "Fine, but you have to take one of your dad's long range walkie talkies and check in with us at least once an hour until you guys go to sleep."

The other Cavers had no trouble convincing their parents to let them go camping, and the night of my birthday we slept in tents on any flat ground we could manage around The Rock.

Part of me would rather gloss over what happened next, yet the story won't make sense unless I lay it out. That night, atop The Rock, under the stars, I lost my virginity to Alicia. The act itself was embarrassing enough that I won't dwell on it, but what must be focused on was what occurred afterwards.

As she lay her head on my chest, I felt a sudden pressure in the center of my heart. Not like that of a crushing or gripping force. No, this was closer to the feeling in your teeth when a popcorn kernel has lodged itself in between them and forced them to spread ever so slightly. It wasn't painful, per se, but it was incredibly uncomfortable.

"Your first coin gathered, little wolf," I heard Alicia say, but the voice didn't come from the direction of her face. Instead, it came from the edge of The Rock to my right. "You've settled into such a peaceful life, despite it all, but that peace is soon to be gone."

I knew the voice wasn't real. I had forgone Ambien for nearly two weeks at that point, and the lack of sleep was getting to me again. When I slowly looked over to where the voice had originated, I saw a rabbit's skinned hide lain in a grizzly display. I ignored it and continued to pet at Alicia's hair. We'd need to climb down to sleep but, for the moment, I couldn't bring myself to move away from her.

The pressure in my heart did not fade, and one weekend morning I went by myself to the mouth of The Oracle's cave. The stone tablet that marked the creature's home had changed.

The third line of the poem was no longer filled with a dull bronze, but instead shone with the luster of gold. From deep within the cave I heard the haunting laughter of a predator who had cornered its prey.

Chapter 21
Haunting Laughter of a Predator

It was the beginning of May, during one of my 'Ambien Periods', that Alicia got her driver's license. She was allowed to get one at fifteen under the pretense of a 'hardship license', since her dad was a single-father who worked chaotic hours, but it was provisional and meant she couldn't drive any of us anywhere. But now, finally sixteen, the 'provisional' fell off and she was more than willing to be the Cavers chauffeur.

Her dad gave her an old navy-blue Jeep Cherokee to drive to and from school, and all of the Cavers started to go with her in the morning and ride home with her if we were able to.

I climbed into the passenger seat and leaned over to give her a quick peck on the cheek, drawing a groan from Allen in the back seat, "It's too early for all of that, you two."

I flipped him off and leaned in to kiss her again, getting a chuckle from Theo, who was sitting in the back of the Jeep instead of one of the seats. He closed his book of campfire stories and threw out, "Like you'd not have your tongue down Jen's throat if you could."

Shannon let out an exaggerated gagging sound, "Can we not talk about my brother making out, please? It's bad enough when I have to hear it coming from his room."

We'd bicker back and forth like that every morning until Alicia put on some song that would draw us all into loudly singing along.

During my "Ambien Breaks" I would often be showered and ready to go to school by four in the morning. I would go over to Alicia's house and– if her dad were already gone– I would sneak in to spend some 'quality time' with her in the morning.

One such morning, near the end of the Ambien break, I pulled back from kissing her to find myself hovering over a desiccated corpse, a centipede crawling from one empty eye socket into the opposite one. The coin in my heart felt hot and moved from discomfort into outright pain.

When I let out a startled yelp, she pulled back and up, wrapping her arms around me to calm me down. It was always such a sudden shift when she flipped from her lustful self to her motherly self.

"Will, what is going on?" she asked, holding my cheek tenderly as I tried to catch my breath.

"It was just one of the hallucinations, don't worry."

A pregnant pause stretched between us. Three silent heartbeats.

"What was it?"

She never asked what I saw. She was the only one that never asked. I blinked and I looked at her with a concerned face, "It… It was bad."

"I can handle it," she promised. I described what I had seen and she shivered visibly, "And how often do you see these things during your 'breaks'?"

I'd stop counting them some time ago. I'd go as long as I

could manage before going back onto the Ambien, dreading the torturous nights of sleep. "Toward the back end? Ten, fifteen a day? Most aren't that bad though."

She balked at how casually I had said it, pulling on her shirt, "Are there any recurring ones?"

I considered lying, felt the burning coin as a reminder of just how involved she was, and figured if anyone should know it was her, "Yeah, a few…"

I told her of The Oracle's cave and the old woman hanging the skins with my friends' faces. When I told her there were a lot of times that I'd see rabbit imagery with her. She seemed more concerned with the description of her being a rabbit than anything else, "Thats… odd."

"Why do you say that?" I asked as I pulled on my own clothes.

"It's just… Shannon always calls me 'Miss Rabbit' when we are alone, but she never does when we are around people."

"Maybe I overheard it at some point, and it stuck with me?"

"No, that can't be right, you've been having these visions–Errrr, hallucinations for longer than Shannon and I have been hanging out by ourselves."

That caught me off guard. Did it have some connection to my nightmares? Did Shannon know something about all of this?

"Maybe I should ask her," Alicia offered.

"No, it's best if I do," I said with a long sigh. "I'll talk to her in class today."

That day in Algebra, my only class with Shannon, I had one of the worst hallucinations I had suffered to that point. Not because of its content, though it was upsetting, but because of its persistence. Most of the time, once I had realized the hallucinations weren't real, it would dissipate. This time, it did not.

As I walked into the room, a massive grey wolf dove toward a smaller canine, though I couldn't place exactly what kind it was at the time, I'd later learn it was a coyote. It fought the smaller brown animal viciously, tearing at it every time it tried to move closer. Behind the wolf was a doe, glistening with silver dew of some kind. In my chest the sizzle of blood on hot metal filled my chest cavity with radiating heat.

The classroom was in complete disarray, empty save for the three animals. Desks were strewn about the battleground, pushed out of the way by the sheer size of the wolf and its foe. The bloody battle continued regardless of the number of times I tried to blink it away. I stood frozen in the doorway of the classroom, some invisible forces jostling me, though I couldn't see anything forcing itself past me.

As I watched the wolf grabbed the coyote by the neck and began to shake it back and forth, showering blood and gore over the entire room with each violent jerk of the limp animal. The wolf threw its rival to the ground and stared at the broken assembly of fur, blood, and bone. After staring at its own handiwork for what felt like an eternity, it began to attack itself, biting at its own legs and any other part of its body it could reach. The deer began prancing about the viscera and headbutting at the wolf as if trying to stop it from hurting itself.

The wolf ignored the pleas of the deer and soon collapsed

from its self-inflicted injuries, going limp from blood loss. I remained frozen in place, unable to process the scene before me when I felt a sharp slap across my cheek.

"WILL!" Shannon shouted in my face, shaking me more.

I grabbed my cheek and looked about in a daze, pockets of students staring at me from their places in the classroom. The teacher had not entered the classroom yet, and everyone was still milling about when I had gone into my trance and, apparently, began whimpering and screaming. Shannon had been trying to shake me out of it for over a minute, but I was non-responsive.

Now that I was aware again, I moved to my desk and slumped into my seat. The students began whispering amongst themselves, a chorus of snickering with the occasional 'freak' rising above the din.

Once the teacher arrived, the class fell into silence. We went into the lesson as normal, but I couldn't focus on the subject, my mind still trying to make sense of the scene I had watched. I could see Shannon across the room staring at me with real concern in her eyes. Once we reached the 'group work' portion of the class, she made a bee-line to sit with me, though the urgency was unneeded. Everyone else was avoiding even looking at me.

"What the hell was that Will?" she asked immediately, whispering the words so no one else could hear.

I looked about nervously, knowing that the outburst would spread around the school before the day was over. I told her of the battle and her eyes watered as I relayed the details. She seemed to recognize the scene and lay a hand over my forearm when I was done.

"I'm… I knew you were having issues with seeing things, but I didn't realize how bad it was."

"It's just sleep deprivation," I echoed from my doctor's assessment. "I'll start back on my meds tonight."

"Will, I don't think it is."

"What do you mean?"

"Just… I'll explain to the Cavers in the field after school, okay?"

I let the topic go and sat silently as she did all the work for our pairing.

After school we all agreed to meet in the field. I dropped off my school bag and immediately headed there, meeting up with Theo at the connecting street. The two of us walked together, arriving after the other three had already picked a shaded spot to sit in.

Shannon told us of her question to The Oracle and the question she asked. It was only later that I would learn that she had left out some important details. Her confession shattered the taboo we had all been holding to not share the details of our questions.

Theo was the first to speak, clearing his throat before speaking. "I asked if there was a way to cure my mom's condition. The Oracle told me there was and that it would save every sufferer of my mother's condition going forward. The treatment was… It was announced three weeks after her funeral."

"Shit," Allen mumbled, looking down at his hands.

I them told of my experience with The Oracle, of the foolish question I had asked. The only detail I left out was about the five coins and the change in the stone's surface. Some part of me knew even then that they wouldn't be able to see the new passage.

Once I was done, I looked over to Alicia, waiting for her to speak up about her experience. She locked eyes with me and shook her head once. I had sworn to her that I wouldn't tell anyone of the marks that proved she had spoken to The Oracle, even though her refusal felt like a betrayal to the Cavers. But what room did I have to speak, having hidden my own details.

"I think Will's hallucinations aren't random. I think he's getting visions related to The Oracle," Shannon said matter-of-factly. It was the obvious line that we all had drawn once the information was all shared. We spoke a while longer, trying in our teenage hubris about ways to fight against the prophecy we had pieced together.

I was the only one that knew the price of changing fate.

Chapter 22
Splinters That Crowded My Heart

Alicia and I had a rough time in our relationship after that. We fought over minor things at times, both of us at our wit's end for different reasons.

I was often irritable, my sleep getting worse now that I knew the visions I received while off of Ambien might be helpful in discovering keys to changing the course we were all on. I would learn how to hold on to the scenes longer instead of forcing them out of my mind sooner, despite the pain of the coins burning in the folds of my heart.

Alicia began growing emotionally distant, seeming to only want me around if it were for sex. As a teenage boy, I was happy to comply when I could, but it never seemed to be enough for her, and she would get angry when I was unable to. The motherly side of Alicia shrank and withered over the course of those two months, and near the end of June she said the words I'd been living in fear of.

"I just think we should take a break for a while," she said. She already looked on the verge of tears, as if I were the one breaking her heart.

"What? What are you talking about?"

"I just... I just think until we figure out The Oracle stuff, it would be best if we... Will, I love you-"

My ears were ringing and I did my best to 'end the vision',

blinking against it the way I used to end them. But it wasn't a vision. It was real. "Please, Alicia, please don't do this…"

"Will, I've already made up my mind," she said, wiping the tears from both eyes.

"What did… What did I do?"

"Will, you didn't do anything wrong. I know when you snap at me it's not your fault, but-"

"I'll go back on Ambien, I promise, and I'll stay on it so I sleep, please."

I will spare you the retelling of the next two hours and the pathetic state that I made of myself. I'll spare you the next two days of wretched crying and ignoring the knocking of the Cavers on my door. I'd also spare you what happened three days after the breakup, if it weren't the next important step in our twisting tale.

I had spent those two days forcing myself to sleep as much as I possibly could. I'd take Ambien the moment I woke up and stumble about the house in a stupor until I passed out on the couch upstairs or while laying in the shower while it rained down on me.

On the third day I finally answered the door for Theo. He didn't say anything, just stepped into my house and shut the door behind himself. He guided me downstairs and forced me to sleep off the Ambien while he sat and played on my PS2. When I woke up, I instinctively reached for my pills, only to find them missing from my nightstand.

I stumbled my way into my living room area, glaring at Theo angrily. "Where are they?"

"Nope, you are done with all of that Will," he said, not even looking away from his game.

I turned off the TV and pointed at him, ignoring how my finger shook, "That is my medication, I'm allow-"

"WHAT?" Theo yelled in his deep voice, throwing the PS2 controller against the wall as he stood up and surged toward me. I stumbled back from him a bit, my fight or flight instincts trying to tell me to run from. I was a head taller than him, but even so, I knew he could easily fold me in a fight, "ALLOWED TO WHAT, WILL, KILL YOURSELF?!"

I stood there dumbfounded, tears suddenly pouring out of my eyes, "I love her Theo."

All the fury left him and he pushed a finger into my chest, "And you will love the next one too Will. And the one after that. But you won't get to those if you keep this stupid shit up."

I crumbled and Theo caught me before I hit the floor, and for the first time it wasn't Alicia that comforted me through my despair. Theo had become my best friend in the Cavers, and Alicia knew that he was the only one that could help in this situation. Allen had taken up smoking pot so often that it was impossible to rely on him for much of anything recently. So, it had to be Theo that confronted me about my withdrawal from the group and talked me through the emotions I was struggling to process.

I learned that she had sent him over after I 'refused' to answer her calls or answer the door, even though the truth was that I had slept through them. She was worried about me, Theo explained. She had told him that she loved me, but it was the wrong time for both of us.

"She'll tell you herself, if you are willing to listen," he

finished, his arm still slung over my shoulder.

"I'll try," I promised.

Chapter 23
Close but Distant

I spoke with Alicia and we agreed to stay friends until we could straighten out our individual issues. I thought to ask her what her prophecy was, to find out the horrible thing she refused to share with everyone else. I didn't, though, deciding to wait until my own problems worked themselves out before worrying about hers.

When school started back up, I still rode with the Cavers to school every morning, though now I rode in the back and Shannon took up my spot in the front seat. No one seemed to notice that I no longer sang along with them. I instead listen to them like an outsider, close but distant. I still went to The Wagon Wheel with them for after-school burgers or milkshakes.

Junior year held even more issues, not the least of which was that my P.E. class was mixed with Seniors. That in and of itself was not a problem, but one particular Senior was an issue.

"What's wrong, Skitzo?" Aiden asked from the center of his cadre of bootlickers. The 'elite' of our school had taken to calling me 'Skitzo' after I had reacted so many times to hallucinations. It never bothered me, the horror of these visions far outweighed anything these assholes could say anyways.

It did bother me that Aiden was calling me 'Skitzo'. "Oh, I was just having a vision of your mom showering. Worst one I've ever had, nearly had a heart attack."

He took a step forward past his circle of friends to press toward me in a 'threatening' way. After you stood in the pitch darkness of a deep cave with some sort of ancient, malevolent being, it was hard to take some scrawny rich boy seriously.

"How about you come over here and say that shit again?"

"What, are you hard of hearing? Surely your dad can afford an ear surgery, right? Or has he gone broke from paying for side action since he can't stand to look at your mom?"

The punch was sloppy and telegraphed from a mile-away. I had gotten into more than one fight in my sophomore year and nearly failed a class because of them. My dad was never mad about me standing up for myself and my friends though, so he continued to teach me the basics of fighting that high schoolers never understood.

I ducked into the wild swing and threw one hard punch into his lower right rib, rewarded with a loud yelp.

And then they were all on me.

Learning to fight only went so far when six boys fell upon you from all around. As I balled myself up to protect my head from the kicks, I heard the combined yelping of a band of coyotes. Something snapped in me and I caught one of the legs that hit my side and with all of my strength and weight I rolled my entire body into the leg.

SNAP

The scream of the boy made his friends all stop and stare, bewilderment pulling them from their blood lust. I was too sore to stand up, so I just kicked off of the ground the best I could to make distance from my aggressors. When the teacher arrived, no one moved, staring at the bone that protruded from the Senior's leg.

"Will, what were you thinking?!" My mom yelled at me from the driver's seat. It was only the second Monday of the school year and she already had to come pick me up. "That boy may never walk again!"

"They were kicking me on the ground! Why aren't you on my side?!"

"I am on your side! Don't you realize they might press charges on you for this?"

"Let them, I don't fucking care anymore!"

"WILLIAM!"

Of course I was grounded, my computer and PS2 taken away, leaving me with nothing but my school books, my growing collection of philosopher texts, and time. I was allowed to work on my school work while the school straightened out how to handle the situation, and everyday Theo would drop off the assignments, though he wasn't allowed to hang out, he always spent a few minutes catching me up on what was going on.

"Kevin's leg is totally fucked, dude," Theo said with a little too much joy in his voice. "And they're saying you bruised Aiden's rib, so he 'can't work out'."

"Wish it was that rich fuck-off's leg I broke," I spat angrily, refusing his name as I had since I swore it off so long ago.

Theo's face had an odd expression, part concern and part pride. "Well, he deserved worse."

"I'm lucky all I got was some bruising on my stomach and back."

He nodded slowly, still studying my face in an oddly intense way. "Well, I gotta go do my own homework. Once you get ungrounded, we all agreed to take you up Shit Creek to throw you a congratulation party."

The hall cameras had caught the exchange, and I was found to be 'only guilty of excessive force', which my dad fought very vocally. I was allowed to return to school a week later, but I was still grounded for another week for how I spoke to my mom when she picked me up. More reading of Kant, Mill, and Nietzsche; just what a depressed teenager needed.

The Friday after I was released from my grounding I was allowed to accompany the Cavers to a 'social' on the stipulation that I was home by 11, and even in my sore state I was excited to be with my friends. I was at the end of an Ambien Period and wasn't too concerned about visions haunting me through the night.

We rode in Alicia's jeep up the four-wheel drive path, and found the ten foot drop off for Shit Creek that was the common meeting place for teenagers, multiple old couches and loveseats left around makeshift fire pits. The so-called 'Falls' was surprisingly calm, only holding two other small groups, one of other high schoolers and one of a group that had graduated the year before. Allen brought more weed than our group could smoke in an entire week, and traded a couple of joints for a bottle of Jack from the graduated students.

I didn't care much for pot and stuck to taking pulls from the bottle of Jack as the five of us made stupid jokes and talked about our plans for the future, all of them ignoring the fact I wasn't supposed to have a future. Alicia, after four or five hard hits on Allen's joint and two or three drinks from the bottle, rested her head on my shoulder.

It felt right, despite everything, it still felt so right. I couldn't find the words to ask her to move away, and so I laid my head over on top of hers. She mumbled something and I tilted my head to hear her better.

"I love you," she whispered, looking up at me with her barely conscious eyes.

I wanted to say it back, but the shard in my heart ached suddenly and instead I looked at the fire. Shannon sat across the fire, watching us like a hawk. She was the designated driver and was the only one in our group completely sober.

Theo walked over to Shannon and pulled her up to dance along to a song blaring from the truck of one of the other groups. And then they were making out.

I blinked in confusion, looking over at Allen who was staring up into the ocean of stars above us. "Hey, what's up with that?"

He blinked and looked at the display, shrugging softly, "They started dating last week, I think. She said something about it, but I wasn't worried about it."

"Huh," was all I could say as I watched them dance about in between passionate kisses. I looked down at Alicia— who had already passed out on my shoulder— and imagined how nice it would've been to dance with her like that.

Shannon drove us home and made sure none of us smelt too bad. I made it to my bed and collapsed into a lump. That night I slept with a nightmare that wasn't a nightmare.

In the dream, I was on Shannon's couch again, kissing Alicia – only it wasn't Alicia anymore. Her face shifted under my hands: soft cheeks sharpening, dark hair bleaching to a coppery red. In a blink, I was kissing Shannon, and I didn't stop.

A distant part of me knew it was wrong, but in the dream it didn't matter. Theo burst into the room and yanked me off her, shouting. I whirled on him like a rabid animal. My fist struck his knee and a sickening snap echoed – his leg buckling the wrong way. Theo collapsed with a howl of pain, but the sound only made Shannon laugh.

She pulled me back to her, eyes glittering with feral delight. I saw blood smeared across her cheek, Theo's or mine I couldn't say, as she pushed me down and climbed on top of me. Theo kept screaming, a high, horrible scream but Shannon moaned like my violence was turning her on.

We rutted right there on the floor while Theo writhed, his bone jutting through skin. The more he screamed, the tighter she held me. Her fingers dug into my back. Hot blood ran down my knuckles. I knew it was a nightmare, but some twisted part of me enjoyed it. I wanted her so badly I didn't care who I'd hurt.

I jolted awake in a tangle of sweat-damp sheets, my heart hammering. The darkness of my basement bedroom felt oppressive, the air too thick to breathe. I'd grown accustomed to nightmares over the past year, but that dream was different. Alien and intrusive in a way I couldn't even articulate.

When Alicia called the next morning, her voice hesitant and concerned, asking if she'd crossed a line the night before, I lied without thinking, reassuring her it was fine. As I hung up, the ache around the coin lodged deep in my heart sharpened into something jagged, reminding me that some secrets hurt more to keep than to tell.

Chapter 24
Like it Used to Be

It was getting close to Alicia's and Allen's graduation, and prom season was getting into full swing. Allen was going with Jen– whom he had dated on and off for over two years. Alicia asked me to go, just so she wouldn't have to go alone. I agreed, but we both agreed that it didn't mean we were getting back together.

She wore an elegant golden dress that complimented her height while also being sleek in its curves. I wore a golden shirt to match it and the two of us danced through the night, staying near Allen and Jen throughout the night. Aiden was elected Prom King with one of his recent trophies winning Prom Queen.

That night, Alicia and I tumbled into her bed. We swore it wasn't like it used to be.

But it was. It was exactly like it used to be.

That was the last time I ever really felt loved by a woman.

Because that night, my mother died in her sleep.

Chapter 25
No Soul Under That Flesh

The feeling of pressure in my chest woke me up, another sliver of stone shoved into the folds of my heart's muscles making everything feel displaced. I knew immediately that something was wrong and sat up in Alicia's bed, eliciting a groan from her. I looked over at her, laying there in a sweaty heap. I did my best not to wake her up as I dressed enough to make the trip home in the humid midnight air.

As I walked the street connecting our roads I heard the scraping and slithering sound of The Oracle in every shadow. The thudding of my heart increased with every step, and by the time I was opening the garage door, I couldn't hear anything over the sound of my own heart thundering in my ears.

I dropped off my suit jacket and kicked off my shoes, hurrying up the stairs. My mom had fallen asleep on the couch watching TV, just as she had so many times before.

"Mom, wake up, I think something is wro-", I said, grabbing her arm to wake her.

If you've never touched a dead body before, I can't fully describe the feeling. Even being dead for less than twenty minutes, the skin felt wrong. It was too cold and rubbery. There was no resistance to my touch that a muscle reacting to touch would give. There was no soul under that flesh.

I always thought that, if I were to lose one of my parents,

it would be my dad. His job was dangerous and he faced that difficult career with a fearless determination. My mom, though, I thought would outlive me. She was cautious and even avoided driving when it rained. She was supposed to be there when I got married one day.

I don't remember the details of the rest of that night. I know I called 911 first and then called dad. He left his work site and was home less than five minutes after the ambulance. I moved about in a confused daze the rest of the night, and my dad fought back his own tears to try and comfort me.

I found out two days later that it was an aneurysm; that she died instantly and felt nothing.

But we were left feeling everything.

I was excused from the rest of the school year and my dad took a three week leave of absence from his work. He did his best to comfort me, but in the middle of the night, when he thought I was asleep, I'd hear his muffled wails.

I took my Ambien enough to sleep through most of the day and night, but the nightmares meant that even sleep offered little reprieve. I knew my friends would try to visit, but I told my dad that I didn't want to see them. He didn't like it but he respected my wishes anyway, turning them away in my place. Just a few years ago I would've given anything for friends like them, but now I was forcing them away, unwilling to break away from my own despair.

Much like an echo is a smaller, weaker version of the original sound, my mother's funeral was an echo of Theo's mother's funeral. I was still in a numb, shambling state when it came, and I remember not speaking to anyone at the service.

A couple of days after the funeral I received a bundle of notes. Each was between two and three pages and was handwritten by one of the Cavers, except the one from Alicia that was closer to ten pages. I didn't read any of them, just leaving them unopened on the desk on my table. I felt disconnected from reality, like I was some sort of specter that was floating from one place to the next but never touching anything.

It was Theo that finally forced me out of my grief-formed stupor, two days before Alicia and Allen were to graduate.

I was laying in bed, staring at the wall, trying to decide if I was still in a nightmare or if I'd woken from it. The distant laughter of The Oracle was now constant and clearer, and it gave even my waking moments a dreary, nightmare-like edge. And then his wide form was in the doorway, leaning against the frame with his arms crossed.

"Hey," he offered softly.

"What- how did you get in here?" I asked, not bothering to move or rise from my bed. I was half waiting for his face to melt off or something of the like.

"You're dad let me in," he said, moving to sit on the foot of my bed. "Said that he didn't know what to do with you. I can smell why."

I'd not showered in- how many days had it been? It didn't matter. Nothing really did. "Fuck off, man."

"I don't think I will, bud. You see, my best friend is in a lot of pain, and I don't want to watch him suffer anymore."

"And what? Are you going to bring my mom back, Theo?" As

soon as I said that, I felt a pang of guilt.

Theo was the only one that could understand how I felt. Alicia's mom had died during childbirth. Shannon and Allen still had both parents, even if they lived separately. But Theo had lost his mother too, and even had to watch her suffer for years until the end took her.

"Does it… Will it get better?" I asked, feeling tears welling up in my eyes already.

"Better? No. But it gets easier to deal with," he said, patting my leg. "And we will help you through it, if you'll let us."

And they did, they helped me recover. It wasn't overnight or anything, but slowly I became more like my old self. I made it to the graduation, even though I didn't feel up to going to the after party at Shit Creek that all the seniors threw.

By mid-June I was meeting up with them on a regular basis again, even if I was quieter and more distant, at least I was there. I had gotten my license already, and my dad took the time to teach me how to use his old truck's four wheel drive. He'd let me drive it anytime, so long as I let him know when I was leaving and was home by curfew.

It wasn't my happiest Summer, by any measure, but I was approaching normal again.

Chapter 26
A Thousand Little Reasons

My senior year was stressful for a thousand little reasons and a handful of larger ones.

Classes that should have been easy were made herculean with my terrible sleep schedule. I'd taken the majority of my "hard" classes in my junior year, hoping to make my final year an easy one. Instead, I was barely maintaining a C average in all of my classes. I wasn't even able to retain the most basic of concepts from Econ and Political Studies, a class I was actually excited for.

It remained difficult to focus even when I wasn't being distracted by the sound of insect legs skittering in the shadowy corners of every classroom. That sound was all too common though, even when I was well rested. I'd be writing a note in Senior English when I'd hear that horrid noise and whip my head around to find a confused look from the student behind me.

Also, I'd often find myself suddenly crying out of nowhere. Some passing thought reminded me of my mother: a turn of phrase a teacher used; the mention of some TV show she liked; some passing smell that reminded me of her. Then I'd begin weeping and leave class without explanation. All of my teachers were understanding, luckily, and none would press me on the outbursts. They had all been warned.

Theo and Shannon both had the same lunch break as me, as did Stephen and Jen. The five of us would eat together and the others would do their best to keep my mood in check, ignoring the way I would occasionally glance over at a corner of the room for a bit too long. Shannon would occasionally lay a hand over my back and act like she had directed me to check something out. When she did this I'd always see a concerned look from Theo, though he never said anything about it.

The two members who graduated took very different paths in life. Allen was working as an apprentice for a carpenter. He picked the job because it was a creative outlet that he could pursue while still getting blazed out of his mind almost everyday.

Alicia, on the other hand, had started attending the university down the interstate. She was going for pre-med and was often tied up with assignments and making it to class on time. She would hang out with us occasionally on the weekends– meeting us at Shit Creek with a bottle of whiskey and whoever her current fuck-buddy was.

I was never really jealous of them, though they always seemed to pick fights with me. After two or three appearances at Shit Creek, they'd finally try shoving me or something. I'd always end up winning the fight, though some of them would get a good hit or two in the scuffle. After I thrashed them, they would pout and leave, never to return. The next time she came to Shit Creek she'd have some other boy-toy to hang on, and the cycle would start over again. I learned how to take some real hits though, and that was a valuable lesson in and of itself.

It got to the point that Theo pointed it out after one of the boys left with a bruised eye and shattered ego, "You know, you could just break up with them instead of having Will beat them up."

Alicia gave a coy shrug, throwing a look over to me. I had already sat down and was wiping the dust from the knees of my jeans. "It's not my fault they are jealous of our history, right Will?"

I looked over at her and gave a toothy, hungry grin, "Of course not."

Sometimes– after the fight– the two of us would fuck in the back of her Cherokee and then grab burgers at The Wagon Wheel while sharing little jabs at the poor guy who tried to tame the athletic giantess. Not always, but more than a couple of times.

And the sex, it was… It wasn't the type of passionate sex we had when we were younger, all full of emotion that we once shared. It was more like some kind of animalistic ritual that left me feeling hollow and tired.

Afterward, when we saw our friends next, everyone acted like nothing had happened. Everyone, that is, except Shannon, who would become very quiet and would refuse to meet my eyes for more than a week each time it happened.

One weekend in November we met at The Rock instead of Shit Creek. We had mostly passed on the torch for the Caver Gang to the younger kids of the neighborhood, and none of us really hung out with them. We also didn't tell them of The Oracle, thinking that it would be best not to involve them in that secret.

As we lay around the base of the giant stone, watching our breath puffing up into the air, a question bubbled to the front of my mind.

"Who was the first of us to go to The Oracle?" I asked, looking over at Allen. He rarely made it to our gatherings, but had made it this time since he had just wrapped up a project for his apprenticeship.

"I was," he offered, taking a drag from his joint while still staring up at the stars. "Why?" The question floated out on a cloud of skunky smoke.

"Who showed you to its cave?"

He went to answer as if it were obvious, but then fell silent. He blinked his bloodshot eyes very slowly and then glanced over at me. "I must be blitzed harder than I thought, I don't remember."

"Wasn't it Nathan?" Theo offered from his spot, leaned against The Rock with the half bottle of Captain Morgan in his grasp.

"No, I showed it to him," Allen said, his unfocused eyes turned back up to the sky. "I'm not sure, but I'll figure it out tomorrow."

I nodded, and stumbled over to Shannon. I didn't realize how drunk I was until I had stood up, and the cool night air felt good on my flushed cheeks. I had taken to drinking more often than I knew I should, but the chittering and cackling always lessened when I was drinking.

I sat next to her and slumped over with my head on her lap. She didn't move or protest, offering her bottle of cheap vodka toward me. I thought about it for a moment before shaking my head.

Alicia watched us from her perch atop The Rock, remaining silent. She was a curly-haired raven passing judgement on all of us.

"Th-thanks for always watching out for me at lunch," I

whispered, doing everything I could to keep the slur out of my words. I think I was mostly successful, as she gave a faint smile and shrugged.

"It's the least I can do," she offered, not looking down at me. From this angle, her red hair looked like a frame of flame around her face. The flickering of the small fire we had made reflected in her eyes as she took another swig.

"You could do less," I argued, still fighting back the slur. "You could join the people calling me Skitzo."

"What, and have you break my leg too?" I winced at the accusation. I knew she was kidding, but it was still hard to hear my friend say it. "Sorry, it was just a joke. I'd never be like them and call you such a vulgar name. I'd come up with something more poetic and impactful."

Allen grunted his agreement, "Ol' Firetwig is good at that."

"Firetwig?"

"Because of my hair and frame." I tried to not be too obvious when I glanced at her rather ample breasts that loomed mere inches from my face. Of course, she noticed and laughed, "He always says that even trees have knots that give them shapes."

I heard Alicia huff and look away. She was a very confident woman, except for in one aspect. I ignored it. "What would you call me then?"

She looked down at me and shook her head, sending her locks of red hair bouncing, "Oh no, I'm not doing that."

"Oh, come on," I argued, elbowing at the leg my head rested on.

"Yeah, give'm sumthin'," Theo slurred from his spot a few

feet away. He was always quiet when he was drunk, and I had nearly forgotten that he was there.

"It's only fair," Allen agreed sagely.

"Ugh, fine. Lemme think…" she said, letting silence fall over our little group, only broken by the crackling of the fire. "Mad-wolf."

The nickname hit me like a hammer. Nothing had ever felt more fitting in my entire life. I could almost hear my mom calling me upstairs for dinner with the name.

"Oh shit, I'm sorry Will." Shannon whispered, wiping a drop of moisture from my cheek.

The tears were so sudden that I didn't even realize I had started crying. I wiped them away and chuckled softly, "No, no, that's a good name. I… I like it. Mad-wolf…"

I leaned up with exactly zero grace, turned to face her the best I could, and kissed Shannon on the lips. Just a quick peck, fast as a lightning strike. I stood up and stumbled away to piss.

I don't know why I had done it, but that little sign of affection reminded me of the kiss that she had suddenly given me in my guestroom, and as I pissed to the side of Beginner's Maw, I thought about all the complex feelings I had built up for Shannon when I was younger, and they all felt fresh again.

"She's a dangerous one, that deer." I heard an unfamiliar voice whisper next to my shoulder.

My alcohol-soaked mind slowed my reaction and I lazily looked over my shoulder, before realizing I was alone. I jumped at the realization and nearly fell over. There was no one there, but I had heard that voice as if it were right next to me. I finished up and shook my head, looking around in the darkness that the small fire had kept away. Was that a chuckle coming from Beginner's Maw?

"Will, let's head back!" I heard Allen call. I returned to the fire and helped everyone pack up. Alicia was the most sober and made sure we all picked up everything we had brought and that we flooded the fire with water from the creek.

The five of us stumbled through the woods back to the field and went our separate ways. Alicia stopped me before I split off to head home. "Come back after you get Theo home," she whispered in my ear before nibbling at my lobe to make her point.

I did as she said. I was young and was still trying to numb all the terrible feelings I had accumulated throughout the past three years. That doesn't excuse the fact that I imagined Shannon the entire time I was with Alicia that drunken night.

Chapter 27
This House Isn't Her

"I'm telling you, man, no one showed me to the cave." I had gone over to see Allen the next day, getting an urgent text from him once I had finally rolled out of bed. It was always so hard to get up during my Ambien periods. He remembered the unanswered question from the night before but still couldn't recall being told about the cave.

He was not handling the slip in memory well.

"Okay, okay, then who from the previous group of Cavers has gone?" I asked, munching on a cheese stick from his fridge.

"I think they all have, but I remember them all refusing to tell me about it," Allen said, rubbing at his temples in frustration. "But I also remember being shown it before they all stopped hanging out with us and showing it to the other members."

I thought about the contradicting memories as I finished the snack, seeing Shannon come from their hallway bathroom, rubbing a towel through her hair as she entered the living room that connected to their kitchen. Even though she was fully dressed, I couldn't help but imagine her getting out of the shower and covering up with the grey towel she worked over her red hair- a blanket of smoke rolling from a damp fire.

"He didn't show us until everyone else stopped coming too," she agreed.

I could dismiss Allen's spotty memory, the guy spent more

time high than sober. Shannon's reassurance lended much more weight to the argument. "So, you think that you, what, just knew how to find it?"

"I don't know man," Allen said from the breakfast bar that divided the two rooms. "I think… I think maybe The Oracle gave me its location, like in my mind?"

"You can't be serious," I countered with a chuckle.

"That thing has some form of fucked up magic, Will, and you know it," Shannon snapped with a defensive edge to her voice. I knew better than to imply anything negative about Allen in front of her.

I held up my hands in a soothing way and nodded, "You're right, we can't put it past that thing to trick a new generation into coming to its cave."

The conversation devolved from there into a series of unproductive guess work. When I left I headed over to Theo's to check on him. The boy didn't handle hangovers very well at all. We spent the rest of the late morning talking about our plans for the rest of the school year and who he was going to ask to the Homecoming Dance, since he was the captain of the Football team and a shoo-in for Homecoming King.

He won it, of course, and the dance was a great distraction from the constant strain I was under. Shannon didn't go to the dance, saying that it wasn't really her 'scene', whatever that meant. I stuck to the outskirts of the dance floor and sipped at punch while milling over the choices of dancing partners. I wasn't exactly popular– quite the opposite, actually– but I was a good-looking guy, and friends with Theo, so my options weren't zero.

I ended up not dancing with anyone that entire night, though I wasn't bothered by that. My mind was still struggling through determining what was and wasn't real at times. At one point, I was sure I saw Alicia at the corner of the gym talking with one of the teachers. When I approached to ask why she was there it was instead one of the other teachers and I had simply imagined it was her.

I got home that night and caught up with my dad for the first time in what felt like months. I found him sitting in the garage, tinkering with a new air-compressor he had installed while I was at Homecoming.

"Hey, how's it going?" I asked as I saddled onto one of his rolling stools.

"Still got all my fingers, so it could be worse," he offered flatly, though he offered me a weak smile that didn't reach his eyes.

He handled my mom's death worse than I did, in some ways, and used work to escape his spiraling depression. When he wasn't working he'd keep himself busy with some project in the garage, and would do his best not to be idle for even a moment. But I would still hear him at times, bundled up in their bedroom in tortured sobs.

"How was the dance?" he asked as he rubbed his hands over a shop-towel. His voice was deep and dull, not the voice of the dad I had come to miss from less than a half year ago.

"It was fine," I said limply, watching him for any signs of emotions. "Didn't dance, but Theo won Homecoming King."

"Good for him," he said with a thin veneer of excitement. He didn't really care.

"Say, dad," I offered after a long pause of silence. "When I graduate, do you wanna move?"

The question seemed to catch him off guard and he looked over at me from the compressor. He studied me carefully before nodding slowly, "We could. Why do you want to?"

"I was just thinking, it might be nice to not be in this house while I went to college." The words seemed weak to me, but my dad seemed to understand.

He let out a long sigh before deflating a bit, "You could go to college and get a dorm."

The thought had come to my mind, of course, leaving the little town behind and running from The Oracle's prophecy. I knew it wouldn't work though, the three Greek Tragedies we had covered in Junior English had beaten that lesson into me. "I was just thinking, it might be good for both of us."

My dad said nothing for a long time, finally looking over at me, his eyes glistening in the garage's fluorescent lights. "I miss her, bud."

I moved over and hugged him, his large arms wrapping around me protectively. "I miss her too, dad. But this house isn't her."

"I know, but I… You're right, we should really move somewhere else, huh?"

I was shocked that he had agreed already, but I nodded and pulled away. "Once I graduate, yeah. Maybe move back west or something."

"I'll look into it, you go get some sleep."

I rubbed at my eyes, realizing that I had teared up at some point, "Yeah. Love you, dad."

"Love you too, bud."

Chapter 28
Everything is About to Change

The rest of that school year went by in a blur, though it was a blur of nightmares and hallucinations. The pattern of Ambien Periods and Hallucination Periods bled together, and I was haunted by the skittering even when I was getting plenty of sleep. I barely made it through my classes, but I did. My dad had spoken to the electrical company in Nashville, and was lining up a job.

I applied to another University that was a bit of a commute from the community my dad was planning to move to on the outskirts of Nashville. I got an acceptance letter to attend the semester after I turned eighteen, but I didn't tell the Cavers. It was hard to think about leaving them, but I wanted to wait until after graduation to tell them.

And then it was time for prom and graduation.

If I'm being completely honest, Prom wasn't overly impactful and was overall very forgettable. At the time, everyone else built it up as the most important night of our teenage lives. It was so mundane compared to so many other points in my life already that I couldn't build up any expectations like the others.

Well, that, and it was just two days shy of the anniversary of my mom's death. I didn't let myself focus on that aspect though.

I went solo and spent the night hanging out with Stephen and Jen, who had started dating a month or so before. Theo spent the entire night being paraded around by the Football team and only stopped by to check on me once. Shannon didn't go, stating the same excuse as Homecoming. So, it seemed, acting as the third wheel for my other friends felt like the only option left to me. I didn't really mind and neither did they.

Graduation was two weeks later and the entire Caver Gang was planning on going to the huge Graduation Party at Shit Creek Falls that occurred every year, including Allen and Alicia. The year before they had passed up the party, given the grieving period after my mom's passing. This year, though, they would make up for it with us.

My dad attended the graduation ceremony, waving proudly from the stands as I marched across the stage– doing my best to ignore the shadowy army of legs that stampeded off the edge of the stage. I waved back at him, took the portfolio with my diploma, and returned to my seat. Once everyone had received their sheet of paper, we all tossed our caps into the air and did our best to catch them.

I joined my dad and Alicia in the stands and hugged them in turn; my father seemed to hold me a bit too long and Alicia not quite long enough. The chuckling of the shadows taunted me once I had the thought, so I pushed the observation away and joined Theo and Shannon, trading congratulations with them and their parents in equal turns. The five of us agreed to meet in the field before heading to the graduation party, and our parents spoke in hushed, knowing tones.

We met up earlier than we had set at the graduation, our excitement for the party driving us to be early for once in our teenage lives. We agreed upon taking two vehicles: Theo and I would take my little truck; Allen, Alicia, and Shannon would go in Alicia's jeep. Alicia's dad had 'forgotten' some booze on the kitchen table pointedly and Allen had secured a huge stash of his favorite strand of pot. He'd gotten into growing his own to save money and was experimenting with growing certain types for desired effects. All it took for him to find initiative was tying it to weed somehow, it would seem.

It was the early evening once we departed, the sun fighting to stay aloft in the slowly cooling sky. Theo rolled his window down to match mine and watched the houses of our little neighborhood slowly roll by. As we approached the stop sign that fed onto the main road he glanced over at me and I saw there was an odd expression on his face.

"What's up, dude?" I asked as I looked for oncoming traffic, leading Alicia's jeep onto the main road.

"I don't know man, feels like everything is about to change."

I'd not told him about my plans to move, but he had noticed that I'd been getting rid of some of my stuff before the move. "Is that so bad?"

"Maybe not… But what about your—" he pulled up short, obviously not wanting to say *death* out loud. "You know?"

My attention returned to the splinters that crowded my heart and caused every beat to feel strained, "I…I'm not too worried. I just want to enjoy the time I have."

"I know, but I don't think running away is going to help."

So he knew I was moving and thought it was to run away from my fate? I could understand that, but it wasn't the case. I didn't contradict him, distracted by the skittering of insect claws over the ruff of the cab. I thought about telling him about the five coins and about the barrage of sounds and sights that made me sure I was heading for something that would change everything.

I thought about being honest with him. But I wasn't.

I ultimately said nothing and we rode in mutual silence, the whipping of the window through my truck our only soundtrack as we approached the backroads that led to Shit Creek and the off-road trail that led to the falls, the sound of our three friends singing loudly in the vehicle behind us causing a weak smile to form on our lips. We wouldn't say anything once we got there. They deserved to enjoy this party, and we did too.

Chapter 29
The Night Felt Full of Edges

The area at the top of the Shit Creek Falls was packed with young adults and older teenagers, an armada of four-wheel drive vehicles lining the sides of the rain-fattened-creek. Some played music while others held countless cases full of alcohol and bodies full of hormones. We parked together and collected our assorted party goods into a large cardboard box that I carried behind the group.

Three smaller bonfires burned on one side of the creek and a single larger one populated on the other. The smaller ones seemed to collect the more strait-laced graduates while the larger one seemed to attract the rowdier party goers. Without saying anything the five of us hauled our cargo across the makeshift bridge to the other side and set up around a weathered patio couch and table that had been abandoned here sometime in the past three months. It was already falling apart, but it was better than piling up on the ground around our box.

Allen sold a few small bags of his cheaper weed to passing partygoers but rolled joints for the five of us from his better stash. Simple, clean, and no need to pass anything around. I took mine and tucked it behind my ear, more focused on the nearly full bottle of Jack Daniels resting in my lap.

We didn't talk much.

The music from one of the lifted trucks throbbed in the

background, bass-heavy and warped by cheap speakers, distance, and the constant murmur of the creek. Laughter burst like fireworks from the other bonfires but never reached our side of the water. Ours crackled low, more ember than flame, and the night felt full of edges. Some sharp, some soft, none safe.

The trees swayed under a breeze that never touched our skin. Shadows drifted over the creek in ways that made me uneasy, like the dark was watching us, waiting for something to shift. Shannon lit her joint and exhaled slowly toward the stars. Alicia leaned forward, eyes fixed on the flames, barely blinking. Theo tapped out a private rhythm on his knee, like he was trying to keep time with something only he could hear.

The longer we sat, the more something inside me began to fray. I kept scanning the far bank. Not looking for anything, just feeling it. Something was coming. Not fear exactly. More like inevitability. Like the earth itself was holding its breath, thirsty for blood.

Even the music changed. The bass, once obnoxious, began to sound like a heartbeat. Heavy. Slow. Ominous.

And somewhere deep inside, something older stirred—a primal instinct. I felt like a lone wolf, catching the scent of danger on the breeze. A pack of coyotes was circling, teeth bared, eyes locked on the weakest link. They didn't see us as rivals.

They saw us as prey.

And I couldn't help wondering which one of us they'd pick off first.

Alicia sat with one leg tucked under her, sipping something neon from a Solo cup. Shannon lounged on the broken armrest of the couch, legs swinging in the air. Theo hadn't said much since we arrived. His eyes kept sweeping the crowd, as if trouble had RSVP'd and was running late.

It wasn't.

I saw Aiden before anyone else. He stumbled down the slope on the far side of the creek, flanked by two guys I didn't recognize. His hoodie was too clean for this place: designer, bright, smug.

He hadn't changed at all.

When he noticed us, his whole face lit up like a spotlight.

He crossed the bridge with swagger, eyes locked on me. His friends peeled off toward the main fire. That left just him.

"Wuh-ell, shhhit," Aiden slurred, lifting both hands like he expected applause. The bottle that he loosely gripped in his right hand poured a mouthful of amber onto the weather-smoothed gravel of the falls. "Did the g-ghost whisperer crawl outta his cave?"

Allen stood halfway, but I put a hand on his knee, stopping him short. "Let me."

I stood slowly. Not with any real autonomy, it was just my body acting on its own protective instincts. It simply wouldn't allow me to stay sitting anymore, with a perceived threat looming so close.

Aiden's wavering attention zeroed in on Alicia. "Hey sw-sweetheart. Still slummin' it with the p-poor kids?"

"Fuck off," she said, deadpan.

He smirked. "You allllways were good with your mouth."

"You need to go-" I started.

Aiden clumsily whipped around toward me, pointing with the mouth of his almost empty bottle. "You got somethin' to say, skitzo? Or you just gonna st-stare at me with that haunted, virgin-gone-sour look you always be carry 'round now?"

I stepped forward. "Don't."

A warning. A single word threat. More than he deserved.

He grinned like he'd already won.

"Don't what? Don't t-talk about how you traded your girl for a bottle, so you don' gotta think about mommy dearest? L-last time Shannon was suckin' me off she told me how b-bad it's gotten—"

That's when I hit him.

I didn't think. I didn't hesitate. My fist snapped forward, raw with intent, and caught him clean across the jaw. A sharp, meaty crack echoed in my ears. He staggered, two wild, backward steps, before slipping in the muddy gravel at the creek's edge and going down hard.

He scrambled up, rage twisting his face, snatching up the dropped bottle like he might use it as a weapon. His stance was all drunken bravado: shoulders squared, chin lifted, eyes glassy and furious.

Allen was already shouting something behind me, maybe to grab a log or a flashlight or to stop it, but his words were shredded by the cackling of a crone in my skull and the sound of skittering insectoid legs.

Heads turned. Someone yelled, "Fight!" No one stepped in. The crowd circled like jackals. They were drawn not by concern, but curiosity. Spectators. Hungry for carnage.

From some distant place, "Stop!" echoed with Alicia's voice. It pierced the noise, high and sharp. But it was miles away and of no concern to the wolves and coyotes.

Aiden came at me like a rockslide: uncoordinated, loud, and impossible to stop. I wasn't scared. I wasn't even angry anymore. I was hollow, save for three coins jingling together in the emptiness of my chest.

I moved. Sidestepping his drunken bullrush was easy. Like stepping out of the path of a swinging door.

He flailed past me, caught nothing but air. That was, until he snagged the hem of my shirt and yanked us both on to the course gravel. We crashed together, all elbows and knees and slipping traction. The wet ground sucked at our feet. He threw wild punches that glanced off my ribs and shoulders, more rage than precision.

We grappled, wrestled, clawed. Not fighters. Wrathful animals.

I twisted free, and in those few ragged seconds, we found ourselves at the edge of the falls.

The roar of the water swallowed the music, the crowd, our breathing. The air felt thick with the weight of inevitability.

He shoved at me.

My foot skidded across the moss-slick stone, and by some miracle—whether muscle memory, luck, or survival instinct, I can't really say—my body rotated with the force and let it pass me. I was safe from the pull of gravity.

He was not.

Aiden's footing gave in and he slipped forward. Hard. One

foot shot out from under him, then the other. He spun, off balance, panic flashing across his face.

His arms flailed, searching for anything to hold. And then…

He reached out toward the person he just tried to murder.

I reached out too, out of reflex if nothing else.

But I stopped. Just short. His hand was right there—maybe an inch away. I could've grabbed it. Could've pulled him back to safety.

But I didn't.

I just watched.

He went over. His body tumbled into the darkness beyond the bonfire's glow: spinning, weightless, and limbs splayed. In that instant, the night itself lunged up and swallowed him, a beast of pure blackness and the indifference of nature.

Aiden's scream ripped loose, high and panicked, then disappeared into the inky darkness right after him.

The average heart gets two-and-a-half billion beats in a lifetime. Mine became a metronome, counting five thundering beats, each one a pulse circling around the sharp, spiraling echo of his scream. Just five of my two-and-a-half billion.

Then the scream was gone. The last sound Aiden Carter would ever make.

The silence that followed was violent in its intensity. The entire world paused. A moment of silence for the dead. I felt a fresh searing metal-sliver work its way deep, *deep* into my heart. A piece of iron to join the other three in their waiting for the fifth.

Somewhere inside, a part of me relaxed. Not because he was gone. Not because he deserved it. But because The Oracle had been right again. The words stabbed into my mind.

One of iron. An enemy slain.

I hadn't just watched him fall. I'd let it happen.

And now, with the weight of that fourth coin anchoring itself behind my ribs, the world made a terrible kind of sense. That was the part I couldn't hide.

It took a single, loud pop from one of the bonfires to shatter the stillness into a million jagged shards.

Someone screamed. A glass bottle hit the ground and burst. Bodies lurched into motion.

Aiden's two friends, the ones he'd crossed the bridge with, stood frozen at the edge of the crowd, mouths agape. One of them took a staggering step toward the falls, as if he could somehow rewind what had just happened. The other turned in a slow, stunned circle, muttering "No, no, no," under his breath like a prayer too late.

Around them, the party fractured. Conversations collapsed into urgent whispers. A girl dropped her drink and backed away, arms wrapped around her chest as she called for help. A group of guys near one of the smaller fires sprinted toward the bridge, drawn by the noise like moths to an explosion.

Some stared at the water. Others stared at me. But no one seemed to really see me.

Allen grabbed my arm, dragging me back from the edge I couldn't stop staring at. His grip was too tight, and his mouth was moving. He was saying something sharp and panicked. I couldn't hear it through The Oracle's malicious laughter in my ears. His bravado had vanished, replaced with real fear, like he'd just realized none of this was a game.

I numbly looked over to see Shannon stumble a step backward, hands pressed to her face. "Oh my god," she kept saying, over and over, the words looping like a broken record. Her eyes were glassy, wild, like she couldn't decide whether to run or collapse. She looked at me once—and flinched as if I were a slathering, bloodthirsty wolf.

Theo was already in motion, instincts taking over. He tore away from the group and bolted down the perilous path that wound its way to the bottom of the falls, one of Aiden's former lackeys trailing behind him. His flashlight beam jittered and jerked, searching for a body he wasn't ready to find. Even from a distance, I could see his shoulders shaking, struggling to hold the whole night together with sheer willpower.

When my eyes finally found Alicia, she didn't move. She stood perfectly still, red cup still in her hand, her face a mask of unreadable calm. But her eyes, they told the truth. Not anger. Not horror. Just quiet, devastated recognition. She didn't look at me so much as through me and in doing so, she saw what no one else had. She saw the relief buried beneath my guilt.

She had finally seen something she'd hoped wasn't real. Something she'd tried to save. And she was crushed by its confirmation.

Her silence wasn't emptiness. It was judgment. Not the loud, angry kind, but the quiet kind that comes when someone finally gives up on you. And coming from Alicia, that made it worse. She was the one who had always tried to understand me, even when I didn't deserve it. The one who reached out when everyone else pulled away.

To be seen like this by her, like I'd confirmed her worst fears instead of proving them wrong, hurt more than if she'd screamed. It hurt more than the fall. Because in that look, I saw the end of something. A line I couldn't uncross. And I wasn't sure there was any way back.

No one said my name. No one asked if I was okay. They just reacted to the sudden absence of Aiden. Like I wasn't part of the catastrophe.

But I was.

And maybe the worst part wasn't what I'd done. It was that I didn't feel broken by it. I felt closer. Closer to whatever end The Oracle promised. Closer to understanding how the pieces fit. And somewhere, in the part of me I couldn't bring myself to look at… I wasn't even sorry.

The rest of the night blurred together.

Flashing lights came eventually; red and blue bleeding into the trees they didn't belong near. Officers pushed through the thinned but still gawking crowd with calm, rehearsed urgency. Clipboards, radios, latex gloves. Someone put a hand on my shoulder and asked me to sit down. Someone else gave me a blanket I didn't remember taking.

The Cavers were nearby, not far from where I sat. Theo was pacing in small, rigid loops, his hands clenched into fists, giving clipped answers to a young officer that was trying his best to not snap at him, and barely succeeding. Shannon sat on a cooler with her head in her hands, answering between sharp, shallow breaths, her voice brittle, a pane of glass ready to shatter if pressed too hard. Allen stood with arms crossed, stone-faced, answering every question with as few words as possible. He stared down the cops like it was his job to protect the rest of us from saying too much.

Alicia… didn't say anything at all. She sat beside the fire, a red cup of contraband lost at some point, and stared into the dying embers like they might explain some dark, hidden truth. A female officer crouched beside her, murmuring gentle questions, but Alicia didn't respond with words, only giving the slightest movements of her head by way of answer. She held herself perfectly still, as if even the smallest motion might make the nightmare real.

I answered their questions, but it felt like I was just reading lines from a script I hadn't rehearsed. My voice sounded wrong in my own ears. It was flat. *Detached.* I told them what happened. How he slipped. How we were fighting. That I tried to grab him.

I don't know if they believed me.

I know I didn't believe me.

They took me home sometime after three A.M.

The Cavers had already been taken away. Theo and Allen had both patted me on the shoulder as they left. Shannon stopped beside me long enough to whisper a fragile farewell.

Alicia didn't look in my direction as she left.

She knew I wasn't really there anymore.

What Three Coins Bought Me:
Allen

Shannon didn't say anything the whole drive back. Didn't have to.

The silence coming off her wasn't empty; it had a shape, edges, a direction. All of it aimed at Will.

I sat slumped in the passenger seat, hands shoved under my thighs like staying still might help. I kept my eyes on the window, watching the firelight ghosts drag behind us in the glass.

She watched the road like it owed her something, as if by staring she could make it blink first.

At the next red light, her thumb tapped the wheel three times, paused, then tapped three more.

She only did that when she was holding something back, when words wanted out so badly they rattled her bones.

I didn't ask.

Didn't need to.

I already knew.

The light turned green and she let off the brake like she'd been holding her breath.

Some of the tightness in her shoulders eased. Not all of it, but enough that she settled back into driving. It was something she could control, something that expected nothing from her. I let out a breath too, maybe I'd been holding it for the same reason.

We didn't speak for the rest of the way, just listened to the tires hum and the heater click off into silence as we passed the "Custom Log Cabin" sales building and the old gas station with the flickering, busted canopy light, both of them familiar ghosts with familiar moans.

When she turned onto our street, the headlights swept across the yards like a searchlight. Everything looked smaller than it had that afternoon when this truck drove in front of them, holding Will and Theo. The world felt… Duller. Like tragedy had drained the color out of the world and replaced it with morose hues.

She pulled into our driveway a little too fast and stopped a little too short; she wasn't used to driving Will's shitbox. Even so, she didn't flinch. She just sat there, gripping the wheel like she needed the car to still be moving under her.

She didn't get out right away. Neither did I.

I thought about reaching into my jacket pocket, about lighting up right then and there. I'd reflexively tucked it away once I realized the cops would be arriving at the scene of… the incident, before the bonfires died out and silence fell after Aiden's final scream as he went off the—

My fingers were already halfway into my pocket before I stopped myself. It didn't feel right to smoke in Will's truck. Even if he wasn't here and would never know, lighting up felt like crossing a line he'd drawn long ago when I first started smoking— like stepping on something sacred, or maybe something fragile.

Shannon hadn't moved yet. Her eyes were still on the dashboard like it might start talking to her if she stared long enough.

I shifted in my seat and pulled my hand out of my pocket. It hovered near the door handle before I let it drop back into my lap, unwilling to pop the fragile bubble of silence we'd inflated around ourselves. I knew I had to say something; the silence wasn't going to break itself.

And she deserved better than this oppressive silence.

"Hey," I said, barely a whisper but heavy enough to shatter the silence I'd thought was solid stone.

She didn't look at me. Didn't move. A deer in the headlights.

I kept going anyway. "It's going to be okay, you know?"

She still said nothing, but I saw her jaw clench in the same rhythm her thumb had tapped out earlier.

"It's okay to worry about Will. None of us blame him. You're allowed to put him first. It doesn't make you a bad person."

Nothing.

"And if you're also… relieved, or happy, or whatever about Aiden—"

That got her. Just a twitch. Not her whole body, only a slight tightening of her fists.

I swallowed and pushed through it. "You're not a monster for feeling that way."

She turned her head. Not all the way, just enough that I could see the bloodshot edge of her right eye.

"You don't know how I feel," she said. There was no bite in it, only weariness. She knew I did.

"Bullshit," I said. My tone wasn't mean or harsh, just truthful. "We've both been down there, with the thing in the dark. We've both heard it, felt it. That thing is a real monster, not you…"

I trailed off. Just left the confession to rot on the dashboard.

Now she knew.

She didn't say it outright or spell out what my words meant, but in a quavering voice she still asked, "When?"

"About three weeks after Will told us," I answered, looking down at my carpenter-calloused hands. *About a week before I stole my first joint from mom's boyfriend.* I wouldn't say that part out loud though. She could do the math, I knew.

Her hand went to the ignition and she finally pulled out the key, her eyes never once meeting mine. Then she slipped out and disappeared around the side of the house to "sneak" in through the basement window, though it hadn't really been sneaking since we left middle school.

I didn't follow.

I just sat there for a minute—one that stretched longer than it should have. I watched the spot where she'd disappeared, as if the dark might give her back so she could comfort me for once.

Of course it didn't; the darkness only ever took from me.

I reached down and let the seat fall back slowly, careful not to startle the stillness away. The latch released with a dull click, the kind of sound that meant something had given up.

It didn't feel like a seat in a truck.

Felt like the cushions of a coffin.

It was Will's coffin, not mine.

We never talked about it after he told us his prophecy, but I knew what The Oracle had told him. I knew how he was supposed to go out: not in a glorious battle or a lover's embrace, but just metal on metal, glass and blood.

A vehicle that would become a twisted metal coffin.

For now, though, the truck offered a small comfort, a reminder of better times, of singing stupid songs too loud and out of key. Even if it still carried the weight of two people who had no words for any of this, it was still Will's truck. And yeah, maybe I should've gone inside, brushed my teeth, pretended tomorrow would be normal. But the truck felt closer to the truth.

I didn't want to sleep. I just didn't want to be awake anymore. Not tonight.

Just a short death. Just until the heat of a June morning brought it too close to a real death.

I was standing in the blackness of the cave.

No lead-up. No walk through the woods. Just the gaping darkness. Cold and wrong and too much for physical reality to understand.

Inside was a presence so heavy and old it could crush even the idea of hope.

I remembered what he said. Hadn't said it out loud since. Whisper-thin like his final connection to a reality before his friend's death sentence.

"How do I save them?"

And The Oracle had answered.

And what a terrible answer it was.

But it hadn't been that awful, shifting voice Will had described. Not the layered one, not the horror-movie hiss. No.

It was Jen's voice. The way she used to say "hey, dumbass"

like it was a term of endearment. The way she talked when she was laying on my chest and pretending the world didn't exist outside my basement.

That angelic voice with all the cruel honesty that the universe could bring to bear.

"You can't, my precious lazy fox. You can only watch."

Chapter 30
Four Burning Coins

The sky was just beginning to lighten when they brought me home.

I remember the crunch of gravel as the squad car pulled into our driveway. The dome light flipped on when the door opened, throwing pale illumination across my scraped knuckles. An older officer, with lines under his eyes that marked him as someone who'd stopped trying to understand teenagers decades ago, walked me to the front door and rang the bell. I could tell, even in my dazed state, that he was just happy not to be the one who had to tell the Carters the news.

My dad answered in gym shorts and a faded college hoodie, eyes going wide and alert in an instant. His first look went to the officer's uniform. The second one drilled into me.

"What happened?" His voice was equal parts concern and apprehension.

"Sir," the officer began gently, "there was an incident last night. Your son was involved in a… scuffle. Another student is currently missing."

The words 'currently missing' hung in the air like a loaded gun on the table.

I refused to meet my father's eyes. My tired mind craved the nightmare-less sleep of an Ambien, and it took everything I had not to collapse into it.

"Is he—are you saying he is responsible?"

"Not at this time, no sir. Multiple witnesses say it looks like an accident," the officer added, glancing at me with unreadable eyes. "It's unlikely, but your son might need to be brought in for further questioning. We've taken his statement, and for now this is being treated as an accident. Once the boy is found, a toxicology report will be run. If it shows he was heavily intoxicated, that'll confirm what most of the witnesses reported. He slipped. There's no indication of intent."

My dad nodded slowly, running a hand through his hair. "Right. Okay. Thank you."

"You should keep an eye on him for a bit. Shock, delayed reactions. If he talks about hurting himself, call us immediately."

The officer's eyes lingered on me a moment longer than necessary, then he tipped his hat—actually tipped it—and turned back toward the car.

We didn't speak. My dad just stepped aside and let me shuffle past him into the house. I don't remember making it to the couch, I only remember waking up from one nightmare to fall back into another. Both paled in comparison to the one I awoke to.

It was late afternoon when I finally stirred. My neck ached from the way I'd slumped into the couch cushions, and the blanket someone had draped over me was half on the floor. My whole body felt carved out and then re-filled with cold smoke and four burning coins.

The living room was quiet, except for the muffled ticking of the old wall clock– the one my mom had insisted on that we both hated. My dad sat in his recliner, chunky work laptop balanced on his knees, fingers paused over the keyboard.

He looked at me with the type of concern only a parent can muster. "Hey sleepy-head," he said, softly. "You're alive?"

I shrugged, but it came out more like a wince. "Barely."

He nodded sagely and then sat his computer to the side. "How do you feel?"

"Sore… Thirsty." The words felt heavy on my tongue. I sat up slowly, rubbing at my eyes more. "What time is it?"

"Little after five," he offered before going to fetch me a glass of water. "You've been out almost all day. I didn't want to wake you."

He waited patiently as I downed the water in one long drought and shambled off to the bathroom. When I returned and slid back on to the couch next to him.

His voice was soft but firm, like he was trying to make the words not hurt but still leave no room for denial. "They found the body around eight hours ago."

I said nothing, frozen like a deer in the headlights.

He continued in the same tone, eyes distant. "Downstream. It was caught up in the roots and rocks past the old boat ramp."

I stared at the hardwood floor's oaken pattern. The words didn't seem real. None of it did.

"They already ran the tox screen," he added gently. "His blood alcohol was through the roof. Something harder, too, but they didn't say what. Wanted me to know that you weren't being investigated any further."

I didn't speak. I didn't move. It felt like even blinking might snap me in half.

My dad rubbed his face with both hands and sighed, then looked at me. I finally noticed how tired his eyes were. He hadn't slept since I was dropped off. "Apparently the Carters aren't going to press charges. There's not going to be a trial. Not after that report. Seems like they're… sweeping it under the rug. Probably going to be a quiet, private funeral. No press. They've already stopped returning the police's calls and are having their lawyers answer any questions."

He paused, like he wasn't sure how I'd take that.

"Why?" I asked, my voice cracking. I needed another glass of water. Or three.

"If I had to guess? Because it's easier for them this way," he said, gently. "Less scandal, less blame, less grief. Maybe. I don't know. But I think… I think they'd rather pretend nothing ever happened than try to untangle it in the public eye."

I nodded slowly. It felt wrong. All of it. Aiden was dead because of me.

My dad reached over, rested a warm, solid hand on my shoulder. "Look, Will. I don't care about legal charges right now. I care about you. I care about what this all means to you."

I swallowed hard. I couldn't look at him.

"You don't have to talk," he said with a gentleness I had only ever heard him use with me and my mom. "Not right now. But when you're ready—when you can—I'll be here. Okay?"

I nodded again, eyes burning.

"Good." He gave my shoulder a light squeeze. "You're not alone in this, son. No matter what happened out there… I'm still here. I've got you."

I let out a shaky breath. It didn't make the guilt go away. But it let something else in.

Something softer.

Chapter 31
It Started With Small Things

It started with small things.

I stopped going out of my way to see Dad when I heard him moving around upstairs. I stopped watching TV in the living room with him while he worked on maintenance reports. I'd eat in my room and drop off the dishes when I knew he wasn't home. I'd pretend I was asleep when he knocked on my door on his way to work.

He didn't push. Just left space for me and reassuring notes on the fridge.

He was trying. I wasn't.

By the end of the week, I was spending more time at Alicia's house than my own.

Her dad was gone, a big work trip in Portland for nearly a month, which turned her place into neutral ground, a limbo none of us had the words to name. The group drifted in and out like satellites just close enough to say they'd checked in. No one asked hard questions. No one asked if I should head home.

Had to make sure Will was okay, right?

There weren't plans, just rhythms. Theo took mornings, headphones in, laptop out, trying to rope me into some anime he was binging. Shannon brought takeout for lunch and looked like she hadn't slept in days. She looked haunted, but maybe also… lighter? I wondered if part of her was glad Aiden was gone, too.

Allen came around dinnertime, like clockwork. Said little. Smoked more. He always brought fresh joints and left with empty bottles, most of them mine. He claimed the same spot by the back door and never stayed long. He didn't say anything about how much I was drinking, but he always took the empties with him, collecting evidence no one would ever see.

And Alicia… Alicia was always there, of course. She never pushed, never scolded, never offered the affection I'd come to rely on. Just a steady presence, more warden than lover now, like I was someone on probation under her watch. We didn't talk about Aiden. Not directly. But every once in a while, she'd look at me with a raised brow. I'd shake my head. She'd turn back to the TV.

Nothing said. Nothing risked.

His name hovered at the edges of everything, like a dark stain on a pristine carpet no one wanted to acknowledge. The closest we got was Theo, murmuring, "Like I should feel bad for him or some shit," one night as he passed me a joint. No one responded. Later, Allen cracked a joke about Aiden's haircut being "finally gone for good," but the silence that followed was sharp enough to cut glass. Even he looked like he regretted it.

Nobody brought him up again after that. Not around me.

I tried to 'earn my keep' in small ways. Took out the trash, washed the dishes one night when I couldn't sleep, but Alicia never acknowledged it or said thank you. She never said much of anything to me. Her eyes sometimes did, though. Quiet glances that held too much meaning. That saw too much. I avoided them when I could.

We were all pretending, in our own ways. Pretending this was just a break between school and whatever came next. Pretending we weren't thinking about that night every time the room got too quiet. Pretending Aiden hadn't fucked off over a waterfall and died.

And I was pretending most of all. Pretending I wasn't the one who let him fall.

It was sometime after two when I jolted awake on Alicia's couch, heart hammering and shirt clinging with cold sweat. The dream had started the same way they always did. Shadows at the base of the falls, The Oracle's voice curling around my spine. But this time, it wasn't her waiting in the dark.

It was Aiden: dripping, broken, mouth hanging open like it wanted to scream but had forgotten how.

I gasped and sat up, blinking against the dim light from the kitchen.

Alicia stood in the hallway, wrapped in an oversized hoodie, barefoot, staring at me, unsure if I was going to cry or scream or both.

"You okay?" she asked quietly. Coldly. Her first words directly to me in three days.

"Nightmare," I croaked, wiping at my face. "Just… a nightmare."

She didn't come closer. Just nodded and stood there, still half-shadowed. Her eyes flicked to the half-empty bottle of Jack that I had already retrieved from the floor where it had fallen when I fell asleep. She said nothing. The silence between us stretched whisper-thin, sharp with the implications of everything unsaid.

"You wanna talk about it?" she asked, finally, voice low but not unkind, the edges of her old motherly tone creeping in.

"No," I said. Too fast. I had already taken the top off the bottle. Shamefully, I recapped the bottle and gently sat it back down "It's fine."

She nodded again, slowly this time, like she was cataloguing the way I said it. Then turned and walked back to her room, leaving me in the dim flicker of the TV's standby light.

I waited until I heard her door click shut. After five heartbeats, I picked the bottle back up.

That was the first night I realized something profound, but ugly: drinking made it easier. Not better. Not good. Just easier.

The dread, the guilt, the dreams… They didn't disappear, but they did dull. Blurred just a bit around the edges. Like someone had taken the knife out of my chest and replaced it with cotton balls and static. The alcohol's warmth slid into my limbs, a thief with a soft touch, curling through my veins and whispering, *You don't have to feel all of it right now.*

I hated how much I needed that whisper. I hated how fast it worked.

The dream would leave me shaking, breathless with my heart pounding against my ribs. But a few mouthfuls later? Everything smoothed out. My breathing would slow. My nightmares would fuzz. The weight didn't lift, but it shifted just far enough to let me sleep through to the morning.

And once I knew that… Once I'd tasted that kind of quiet, manufactured or not, I couldn't unknow it. I didn't even try.

Weed helped, too. The next time Theo passed me a joint, I held it longer, let it sink in deeper. It didn't hit the same way. Not warm, not numbing, but soft. Quiet. It turned the sharp edges of my guilt into static fuzz and hollowed out the part of me that screamed at night. When I combined the two, alcohol's burn with weed's float, I found something dangerously close to peace.

If I got the timing right, I could bypass the nightmares entirely. I'd pass out early and heavy, and wake up the next day without having to relive Aiden's broken, dripping face hovering in the dark.

It didn't make me happy. Didn't heal me.

But it made me quiet. And at the time, that felt close enough.

It happened a few nights later, after Theo had gone home early and Shannon bailed last-minute with a text about a family dinner. Allen hadn't shown up at all. It was just me and Alicia, and the silence between us felt louder than usual.

It was barely past eight and I was already half a bottle in. I was in the middle of rolling my own joint– I had already smoked the two that Allen had left the night before– when she finally spoke.

"You've been high or drunk for nearly three days straight," she said without looking at me. Her voice wasn't angry, just tired. She sounded so, so tired.

I shrugged. "It helps."

"It helps what?" she replied, still not meeting my eyes. "Passing out? This is the most lucid you've been in two nights"

I lit the joint pointedly, inhaled deep, held it too long just to spite her, and exhaled with soft, muted coughs. "Is this the part where you start to lecture me?"

"No," she said, finally turning toward me. Her face was

unreadable, but her eyes weren't. They were full of something between concern and disappointment. "This is the part where I ask if you even want help."

"I don't need real help," I snapped. "I need everyone to stop acting like I'm supposed to fall apart on a schedule."

Alicia flinched at that, just a little, and something in her expression closed. "No one's asking you to fall apart. I'm just—we're just worried."

"I didn't ask anyone to be," I muttered, taking another drag from the shittily wrapped joint. I got up and began pacing the living room like a caged animal. "You think I don't know what's going on in my own head? You think I don't know what it looks like?"

"I think you're scared," she said, gently. "And instead of facing that, you're trying to drown it."

I laughed, but it was hollow. "You want to talk about being scared? I'm the one who watched him fall. I'm the one who keeps seeing his face when I close my eyes. So don't sit there and pretend you get to tell me what I'm allowed to do to make that stop."

"I'm not pretending anything," she said, rising from the couch now. "I'm just trying to keep you from burning yourself down."

"You mean like you're allowing me to stay here out of pity? Or because you're scared I'll throw myself off the falls next?"

That one landed too hard. Her jaw tightened. She crossed her arms, suddenly cold again. "No. I'm letting you stay here because I care about you. But if you'd rather spit that in my face, go ahead, get the fuck out of here."

The silence that followed was like ash: heavy, still, suffocating.

She left the room without another word and slammed her door pointedly. I started to pack my backpack and ignored the sound of her restrained crying as I left.

I headed to my house, slipping in the front door instead of using the loud garage door.

The house was quiet when I let myself in, and I moved carefully through the dark. Dad's keys were on the hook, but his bedroom door was shut, and I could hear faint snoring inside. He'd be up within two hours to head to work.

I didn't wake him.

Instead, I headed downstairs to my bathroom and turned the shower on as hot as I could stand it, letting the room steam up and fog the mirror. I stood under the spray for longer than necessary, watching pale lines of steam rise off my arms like ghosts leaving the body. I was still on the edge of being drunk and stoned, unable to tell how long I stood there, but some part of me knew I needed to head out if I was going to dodge my dad.

I scrubbed the grime off my flushed skin, realizing I hadn't showered in nearly five days. Days of drinking and smoking rolled off of me, and I had to admit just how bad I must have smelled.

By the time I dried off and changed into a clean outfit, I felt a little more human and teetering dangerously close to sobering up. Just enough to realize I was getting too sober for comfort.

I stepped into the hallway and froze. My dad was leaning against the frame of the bathroom door, arms crossed, watching me like he'd been standing there awhile.

"You've been gone," he said. Not accusing, just stating it.

"Yeah," I muttered. "Had to get out for a bit."

He didn't nod. Didn't say anything at first. Just looked at me with that same worn-out stare he always wore these days. Then: "You've been disappearing, you know that?"

I looked down at the towel draped over my shoulder. "I've just been out."

"I know," he said, rubbing the back of his neck. "And I get it. With everything that's happened… I know it's a lot. But the way you've pulled away from me… from this place… it's not just grief anymore. You're cutting everyone off. Including me."

I shifted my weight, already calculating how I could end the conversation. But he kept going.

"You probably don't even remember, but when you said you were done with your old name—when you told us you wanted to go by Will—it was the week we moved here."

I blinked, caught off guard. "Yeah. I remember."

"Your mom cried that night," he said quietly. "Not in front of you. But she did. She said it was your name to claim, and she meant that. But it still hurts."

He paused. Not waiting for me to respond. Letting it sit there like something we both had to look at.

"And it hurt me, too," he added. "Because that name… it was mine. And my father's. And yours. We gave it to you because it meant something to us."

I didn't answer.

"I guess I always thought maybe you'd come back to it," he

said. "Eventually. When you are ready. But now…"

He let the sentence trail off. I kept my eyes on the floor.

After a moment he took a shallow breath and stepped aside. "You're not a kid anymore. I get that. But you don't have to do this alone. Even if you don't want to be like me… I'm still here."

I said nothing. I should have said something, but I didn't.

I should have hugged him.

He waited for another heartbeat, then walked off down the hall. Didn't slam his door. Didn't ask where I was going. Just left.

He should have hugged me.

I grabbed my old jacket from the coat rack, tucked my toothbrush and deodorant into my bag, and slipped back out the front door without looking back.

I headed to Allen and Shannon's.

Chapter 32
The Fifth Coin

Allen answered the door with a grunt and a nod, then turned and headed downstairs without a word. That was enough of an invitation. He was clearly already blitzed.

Their basement was surprisingly put-together. Cleaner than I remembered, maybe cleaner than I deserved. A big sectional framed the room, worn but comfortable, and a newer flatscreen on an entertainment stand played some old cartoons on mute. A warm lamp glowed in the corner, soft and golden, chasing off the usual basement shadows. The smell of incense hung in the air, musky and herbal.

Shannon was curled up in the corner of the couch with a blanket over her legs and her hair piled in a loose bun. She looked tired, but not surprised to see me.

"Well look who it is," she said, raising an eyebrow. "Was wondering if you were gonna show."

"Why's that?" I asked as I settled into the side of the sectional Allen hadn't melted into.

"Alicia called and said you left in a pretty big huff," Shannon said carefully, then shrugged. "What brings you here?"

"Figured I'd crash the party," I offered lamely.

"You're always welcome here, Mad-wolf." Allen chuckled from his spot sunk into the couch. The name stung for some reason, but I ignored it.

"Well, he's already off to the races. You want a hit from his new strand?" Shannon asked, not even glancing at Allen.

I nodded a little too eagerly. She unfurled herself from the couch and fetched a large bong from the other side of the room. She packed it quickly and turned it toward me, already flicking the lighter.

We each took two long drags and melted back into the couch beside each other. I could already feel the cotton spreading through me, padding the hollow inside of my chest where the coins bounced and rattled. Shannon let out a blissful sigh and nodded softly. "He grew a good one this time, for sure."

Allen gave a low grunt of approval, eyes half-lidded, arms folded like a king at rest. "Told you. I've got the Midas touch."

"Yeah, yeah," Shannon said, reaching across the table to pluck the lighter. "You've got the Midas lungs too. Go turn into a statue upstairs before you pass out down here again."

Allen groaned but didn't argue. He pushed himself up with the slow, exaggerated movements of someone stoned out of his skull and made his way to the stairs. At the bottom step, he turned back and pointed a lazy finger at me. "Crash here if you want. You know the drill."

Then he was gone, footsteps dragging upstairs like someone underwater.

Shannon waited until we heard his door creak shut. Then she stretched and stood like a lazy cat, flipping on one of her grungy CDs. "You eaten?"

I blinked. "Not since… I think I had breakfast?"

She gave me a look somewhere between amused and

exasperated. "Jesus, Will. You're hopeless when you're starving."

She disappeared into the kitchenette. I heard her rummaging through the fridge, the microwave humming a minute later. The air smelled like weed and incense and cheap frozen pizza.

"You like pepperoni, right?" she called.

"Yeah. Thanks."

"Don't thank me yet," she said, grinning around the corner. "I'm not feeding you out of kindness. I just don't want you puking on the couch."

I laughed. Real and unforced. First time in days.

She returned with two paper plates and handed me mine before curling back into her spot. We ate in silence for a few minutes, the kind that's comfortable but charged, like something waiting to surface.

After we finished the admittedly bland pizzas, I stood to toss the plates. I returned to find her tilting the bong toward me. "Round two?"

"Yeah," I said, my voice low and distant. "Why not."

She lit it, inhaled deep, held it. When she passed it to me, our fingers brushed. I didn't pull away.

I took my hit slower this time, let it crawl through my lungs, blur the last sharp edges in my head. When I exhaled, I felt the quiet settle over us again.

Shannon leaned her head back, eyes half-lidded. "Do you ever think about how weird it is?"

"What is?"

"All of it. What happened—how fast everything changed."

I didn't answer. I didn't need to.

After a moment, she continued more quietly. "It's selfish, but… I was jealous of you two. You and Alicia."

That made me glance over. Her face was unreadable in the dim lamplight. More shadows than expression.

"I didn't want to be," she added quickly, "but you guys had that thing. The way she looked at you… I don't think she's ever looked at anyone else like that."

"What do you mean? She had plenty of fuck-toys, didn't she?" I asked. The high blocked out any jealousy from the statement.

She laughed softly, without humor. "Not like you, no."

I didn't know what to say to that. I stared at the cartoon flickering on the screen. The melancholic song seemed to bleed into the animation like spilled ink.

"I'm not trying to start something," she added after a pause I hadn't noticed. "Just… figured you should know."

"What were you jealous of though?" I asked, if only to avoid thinking too hard about that kiss in my guest room.

She didn't answer right away. Just played with a Zippo lighter, flicking the flame on and off.

Then, softly: "I wanted someone to look at me the way you looked back at her."

That hit harder than I expected, even through the haze. I turned to her. This time, she met my eyes.

"Back at The Rock," she said, barely a whisper, "when I was dating Theo—when she laid her head on you? You two looked at each other like nothing else existed. I kept wondering if anyone would ever see me like that. If I could ever matter that much."

"You mattered to Theo," I said, though it rang hollow.

She snorted. "Theo needed me. And only for a little while. That's not the same."

She shifted closer on the couch. Just a few inches. I didn't move.

"I kissed you because I wanted to feel chosen," she said, eyes glinting, more predator than friend. "Even if it didn't mean anything to you."

I didn't say anything. Because it had meant something. Not enough. But something.

She leaned in a little further, voice low. "I never hated Alicia. I just... wished I could be her. Even for a night."

Her knee touched mine. The silence between us turned fragile and sharp.

"You don't have to say anything," she murmured. "I'm not trying to manipulate you. I've just... been there, Will. I know what it's like to want to turn it all off."

She reached up, brushed her thumb against my jaw, featherlight. "So, if you want quiet tonight... I won't ask questions."

I swallowed hard. The warmth from the weed had turned into something heavier. Not comfort. Just leaden weight. Like I was sinking into the couch, and her hand on my face was the only thing keeping me from vanishing. I didn't pull away. But I didn't lean in.

Because what I wanted, I finally knew, wasn't Shannon. It was Alicia. And that thought broke something open in me. Not gently. Not like a lightbulb flicking on. More like the glass shattering in your hand, all blood and pain.

I loved her. God, I still fucking loved her. And I hated that. Hated that after everything, after the silence, the coldness, the way she looked at me like I was someone she didn't recognize, she still had that hold on me. Like a hook beneath my ribs.

She didn't want me anymore. Not really. She wanted me better. She wanted the version of me from before the falls, from before that cave broke something in me.

But that Will was gone. I'd let him fall too.

So what did it matter now? What difference did it make who I kissed? Who I let see my broken pieces? If Alicia couldn't love the version of me that was left… Well, maybe someone else could. Even if it wasn't love. Even if it was just for tonight. Just for the quiet.

My breath shook. I hated the person sitting there. I didn't say yes. I didn't say no. I just didn't stop her when she leaned in to kiss me.

It was different from last time in every way. Not impulsive. Slow, aching. She kissed me like she'd been waiting an eternity for it.

I'm not going into details. But as we fumbled to undress each other, I felt the pressure start—not a stab this time. A slow push of bitter, heated metal slipping inch by inch into my still-beating heart.

The fifth coin.

She rode me into numbness. And I let her. Just for the quiet. Just to forget.

What Three Coins Bought Me:
Alicia

I slammed the door, not because it made me feel better. Not because I wanted to hurt him. Because it was the only sound I knew I could control. If I tried to argue or plead with him I would lose any amount of control I still gripped on to.

The door hit the frame harder than I meant and I heard the pictures in the hall rattle on their nails.

The picture. The ones of me and mom. Before I heard the words that would lead to her—

I waited, locking away and ignoring that thought where it had been before. I stood with my back against the door, listening for his footsteps. Hoping, foolishly, that he might come and speak first.

Instead, I heard the front door open. A pause. Then the creak of it closing. Careful, like he didn't want it to echo. Like even in the inebriated mess that used to be Will, he still wanted to be gentle.

For me. To protect me from—

Then the silence. The kind that settles into sedimentary layers. Thick. Unmoving. Uncaring.

I waited three short breaths.

Then three more, halting.

Then three more, shaking.

Then I finally slid down the back of the door and let myself fold into a pile of branches on the carpet, the tall tree of a woman finally felled by the woodsman ax.

No sobbing. No sounds. Just the quiet collapse of a young oak.

I sat there until my knees started to ache and my palms felt numb from pressing into the floor.

When I got up I opened my door. Slowly. Carefully. Like the room might break if I broke the seal too quickly. I peered into the hallway, the kitchen, the living room.

He was really gone. He'd really left.

I made it to the bed before I collapsed, but just barely. I didn't cry. That part would come later, in pieces. Like everything else I tried to feel. Small chunks that refused to fit neatly inside of me like he did that first time. when I gave him my— when I took his—

I cried the hardest I had since the funeral. My mother's funeral, to be clear. This neighborhood has had so many at this point that I know there is a need to be specific, even in my own mind.

I don't know how long I lay there before the memories came back to me.

Not the usual kind. Not images or a dream. Just the weight of them. Like the smell of rotting leaves and decomposing flesh rising through the floorboards. Like a breath I hadn't taken yet but already knew would fill my lungs with knives.

My eyes were dry, but my mouth was sour. I shifted in the ocean of my empty bed like maybe if I moved just right, I'd bump into him again. That the thought wouldn't stick.

But they did. They always did.

I was twelve when I asked.

Four years after the funeral.

One year before Will arrived like a breath of clean air after breathing smog for five years.

Back when silence had already become a second skin, and I'd stopped expecting anyone to help me peel it off. They only expected me to help them when they hurt, but never thought to check if I was hurt.

It wasn't a spontaneous decision. I'd thought about it for months. This wasn't a split-second decision. I knew the answer before I'd even ask the question.

Had known it since the first time I heard my dad say it wasn't my fault in that voice that meant he thought it might be. 'She loved you more than anything.' and 'This wasn't about you.' he had said.

But she left. She still left.

So I wanted confirmation. I needed to know.

I went with those three stupid coins to the cave. I spoke to the monster I swore to myself I would never seek. The one I made Allen promise to never speak to.

More than anything else in the maze to reach the beast, I remember the air.

Not the chill. Not the smell.

At least, not exactly.

But the way it tasted.

Like the flavor of a decaying tree trunk's breath.

The kind of rot that comes in late autumn, just before the winter's cold hardens everything.

I wasn't scared. Not then. I'd moved past fear when I was eight and watched my mother's casket disappear into damp soil. Scared is for people who think something bad might happen. I had already faced that inevitably. I stepped into the dark and didn't flinch from its chilled hush.

I just stood there until the silence stopped feeling empty and started to feel expectant. Something waiting outside of view.

Then I asked.

Quiet. Flat.

Like reciting the question a teacher expects someone to ask, even when everyone already knows the answer. "How can I ever be loved enough to not be left behind?"

My words were a litany. The reply was a foregone conclusion. There was no echo. Just a hush, a too-long held breath. A pause hung brittle with the impending laughter of a malicious being, the darkness itself amused that I'd even bothered to speak into it.

Then the exhale. A single bark of a laugh. No words, just the presence before me reveling in my stupidity. Then another. Before the being gained control of its hateful mirth.

It was too close, too warm; the horrid laughter being restrained just next to my ear. It knew a mean-spirited joke, and was overly excited to share it with me.

And then it finally spoke. And it was her voice.

My mother's.

Not her strong voice. Not the one that used to sing with. The broken one. The version I only heard when the pills were still dissolving and the vodka hadn't hit yet. "The rabbit loses her mother…"

I went deathly still. A rabbit frozen by the snap of a distant twig, hoping the predator didn't see her.

But it did. It already had its teeth sinking into its supple fur.

The shape of The Oracle shifted in the dark. I couldn't see it. But I could *feel* it. Tall. Then small. Then sideways. Then too big to be anything real. But it never touched me. It knew I wouldn't run, it didn't have to hold me in place. I was too scared of the answer.

The voice changed again. My father's voice now, the one before he straightened back out. The one soaked in guilt and whiskey, slow and bitter that his wife took the coward's way out. "Off she hops into the sweet hush of death, where nothing can hurt anymore."

Then Theo's voice, soft and unsure. A note of longing that I'd only recognize later, but not from him. "The kit stays behind, of course. And blames herself."

Shannon, whispering to me in eighth grade. The day I wouldn't say why I missed school. "She wasn't *enough* to make the mother rabbit stay."

Then someone older. Maybe a thirty-something Allen. Or maybe just a stranger. It was the kind of voice that wears itself out protecting everyone else. "She makes herself useful. Becomes the mother she lost, for all the little creatures of the forest. Not one of them thanks her."

And then—

Will's voice.

The one he used the first time he said he missed me. The one from the night he cried into my hair. The one from after.

"Then, oh, then—she finds her wolf."

I didn't know that voice back then. Not when I first heard it. But now I do.

I turned to run. I swear I did.

But my legs wouldn't move. The Oracle didn't hold me in place. It didn't need to. I stayed. Because I had to.

Then it was my own voice. Younger. Hopeful.

"She wants him."

Another layer of it. Older now. "She tames him."

Then older still. Tired. Ashamed. "She feeds him scraps of warmth in the dark."

The voice returned to Will. Not the sweet one. The broken one. The begging one.

"She let him be closer than anyone… but never close enough to matter, she lies to herself."

Then Shannon's voice. Bitter and sharp, tinged with jealousy. "She keeps him hungry—and pretends that's love."

A prolonged silence. Another held breath. Longer the silence stretches until it is cracked with a hissing exhale. Breath.

And then it spoke again. Not through any voice I knew. Not anyone. Not anything that could be real anywhere else. It was just The Oracle itself: crinkled parchment, reptilian scales, and hatred for all those that had forgotten it. "And when he finally needs her—when he breaks—she becomes the thing she feared most…"

This time it wore my mother's voice again, because that is what it was, a costume to better play the most hurtful character for each line delivered. This time, it wore the skin of my mother from when I was younger. Softer, even. Before everything went wrong and she refused to get out of bed. "The mother who disappears." And then, gentler still. Mocking. Like reading a bedtime fable. "Little rabbit… You wanted to know if you could be loved enough?"

A pause.

Longer than all the others rolled together. Long enough to hurt like lungs begging.

Then the truth. The real voice. Not a whisper. Not a shout. Just certainty.

"Even if you were… you wouldn't know it. And by the time you did…"

I was already running from the cave. I could feel tears cutting down my cheeks. I could feel dirt beneath my shoes, and night above me, and breath tearing through my throat.

But the voice followed me. Closer than sound, in my bones. "…the one who loved you would already be gone, forgotten."

Chapter 33
Cold Certainty

The morning was colorless. Not gray, not yet, but the kind of pale-blue hush that clung to the world just before sunrise. Dew slicked every blade of grass and turned the field into a mirror for the half-formed sky. My sneakers soaked through almost instantly, leaving my feet damp inside. I didn't care.

I hadn't slept. Not since Shannon fell asleep on her sectional next to me. Not since I let go of the last part of me that could still pretend I was innocent. I had slept with her, not out of love, but out of anger and a twisted sense of self-preservation.

The high had long worn off, but a resounding numbness still lingered in my chest. If anything, I'd worn it as skin through the night, pacing the dead-silent neighborhood until the dark began to lift enough for me to disappear into the woods. And now I was walking back toward that unforgiving maw. Back to where my life had started to fall apart.

The trail to the clearing felt shorter this time, but not easier. There were no birds yet, just the sound of my own footsteps and the muted babble of the creek I followed. The air had that early morning cold, not harsh, but enough to tighten my chest with each breath. I was exhausted from too little meaningful sleep.

My hands were shoved deep in my jacket pockets. I didn't need to check. I wasn't carrying them, not really, but I knew I had them. Felt each one like a knot beneath my ribs. Gold. Silver.

Copper. Iron. Copper.

I was surprised to find that I wasn't scared as I drew ever nearer. That surprised me more than anything. There was no panic this time. No anticipation. Just the cold certainty that this was where I needed to be, and that this nightmare would soon be over, one way or another.

The clearing came into view, still cloaked at its edges in the night's deeper shadows. The trees that formed a ring around the mouth of the cave seemed sorrowful at my approach, their branches heavy with condensation, like the forest itself was holding its breath before a gentle weeping.

And there it was. The stone.

I stopped before it. The engraving caught the faintest edge of light, just enough to make the poem glint. It was something alive, four lines each reflecting a different metallic hue. I didn't read it again. I didn't need to. I knew every line by heart.

Instead, I reached up and placed a hand against the stone as I passed it. Its surface was damp and cold, but as solid as a cornerstone of reality. It felt too foundational for such a mystical place. A part of the universe's undeniable makeup, somehow older than the earth it stood upon.

"Five coins," I scoffed, more to myself than anything else.

And then I was past it, pressing into the waiting darkness, and the deeper darkness that waited deeper still.

The cave swallowed me whole. No threshold. No ceremony. Just one step forward, and the world behind me ceased to exist. The blackness didn't just block out light, it erased it. It made light a forgotten concept that had never *really* existed.

I even looked back, once. Nothing. Just inky darkness that challenged me to argue with its claim of eternity. I already knew that I was beyond the point of no return when I first stepped in, so saw no point in trying to fight against such a steadfast element.

So, without delaying further, I moved forward with my left hand pressed lightly to the wall. The stone was clammy, not just damp, but slick with a cold, sticky moisture that clung to the skin, sweat turned stone. Not condensation. Something older. Something alive.

Each time my palm pressed to it, I swore I felt the faintest give, like touching flesh too long in the grave. The wall didn't support me; it fed on me. Drew from me.

But the air was worse.

It wasn't still. It was held. A single breath, sucked in long ago and never exhaled. The cave hadn't breathed in centuries, and now I was inside its lungs. The air slid down my throat like heat from a sealed tomb. Damp, warm, close. It tasted of rot and silence. Of lungs that had long since collapsed. It didn't smell like death. It felt like it.

Stalling would do no good. I pressed deeper.

The tunnel constricted, shape becoming irregular, its walls wrinkled like a clenched fist around me. There was no rhythm, no repetition to the turns now. Just bends and bulges, sharp angles and narrowing gaps. No pattern to follow. No sense to be made. Or maybe I was just too tired to make sense of it.

My spine curled. My knees bent. My feet dragged. I moved like a marionette whose strings had been stretched too thin. When the ceiling dipped low enough to press into my shoulders,

I crouched without complaint. I had surrendered long ago. This wasn't defiance. It was muscle memory.

My footsteps made no sound. The ground swallowed everything. No echo. No crunch. Just the rasp of my breathing and the slick drag of my hand along the stone.

The walls pressed tighter.

At a chokepoint, I had to turn sideways. My shoulder scraped. My ribs caught. My breath hitched. The passage squeezed me like a throat. I wasn't walking through rock anymore, I was being digested.

Still, I pushed forward.

The corridor sagged into a slump. I dropped to a crouch. Then to my hands and knees. The ceiling grazed my back. The floor curved unevenly, forcing me to crawl sideways at times like a crab. My limbs ached. My lungs burned. The air thickened.

It was the same breath, older now, wetter. As though the deeper I went, the more ancient the exhale. There was no fresh air left. Just that same single inhalation, held too long, turned sour in the cave's forgotten chest.

The walls began to pulse with condensation. Droplets bled down over stone in miniature rivers, tears of some countless prior victims. One ran down onto my hand as I crawled. It was ice cold. Another followed. Another. Then a bead of blood from my knuckle as I scraped a splinter. I didn't stop. Just wiped it on the wall and kept going.

It could have my blood. It had already taken everything else.

Another bend. Another choke. My shoulders touched both walls now. My legs cramped. My jaw ached from grinding my teeth in my sleepless frustration.

And still, I wasn't afraid.

That was the terrifying part, how not scared I was. The cave could close in. It could collapse. It could swallow me whole and leave no trace. And I wouldn't even scream.

There would be no panic. No flailing. Just an ending.

But the cave didn't end.

It opened.

Not with a gasp. Not with relief. Just a space. Sudden, cavernous, and empty, but still just a space. Another hollow place to occupy with my hollowness.

I stood for the first time in what felt like hours. My spine cracked. My knees wobbled. My head tilted back toward a ceiling I couldn't see. The darkness stretched, silent and endless.

I didn't move. I just stood there, breathing a lungful of cool air that had waited centuries to be inhaled.

The sound of wet leaves dragging across stone whispered in the dark.

Then came a voice. Just behind my right ear. Soft. Sultry. Gentle. Alicia.

"You've returned, my brave little wolf," her sweet voice cooed, the lightest of touches running over my scraped and bloody forearm, mirroring how Alicia had worried over my injury that first day I met her.

The horrid creature—the one that had set me down this path four and a half years ago—was ready to take my final payment.

Chapter 34
Most Bitter of Questions

The being did not wait for me to reply. It continued in another voice immediately, this time a deep masculine rumble that came from in front of me and vibrated in my bones, my father's sternest voice. "And not empty-handed, it would seem."

Fingers, far too many fingers, brushed the back of my neck, featherlight and teasing. Then they were pressing harder and harder onto my skin, the fingertips turned coarse as sandpaper. I was too tired to flinch away from the abrasive texture.

The air didn't move. The cave didn't echo. But the darkness breathed over me. It pressed against my skin like a mouth against glass.

"You took so long to gather them," came the next voice. This time it was Theo's. It sounded casual and tired, like he'd just woken up or had put off sleep far, *far* too long.

"Almost thought you'd forgotten."

A different set of fingers slipped down the back of my spine, touching me in an alien and unfamiliar way with a texture that felt wrong. Like the top of its nails, maybe? Or the inside of the finger, as if the joints had bent the wrong way. I couldn't tell, it didn't matter. They didn't linger long.

I remained unmoved and silent.

"And yet," said Shannon's voice, sharp and amused, "he still comes back, dragging his shame behind him like a broken tail.

Truly, a mangled little wolf."

Dozens of voices began to stir in the dark. Not words yet, but the intent of words. A whisper-thrum, a thousand breaths forming syllables just beneath hearing. The cave filled with the noise of almost-speech.

Then one voice rose from the tangle, loud enough to pin me in place: my own voice.

"He thinks he's so worthy—so ready."

I swallowed. My tongue felt foreign in my own mouth. Had it stolen my voice? Could I not speak out? Did I care?

Another brush of movement, reptilian skin, running along my jaw like a mockery of a lover's touch. This time the beast didn't even try to sound like someone I knew; just some raspy mixture of tones and syllables.

"I wonder," the voice croaked, cracking like ancient bark and dried bones, "if he even remembers what he came to change."

"I do," I whispered. My voice was still my own, even if I could only raise it in such a quiet way. "I have them."

The breath of the cave rushed past me like a sudden typhoon, and the taste of pre-rain air filled my nostrils as I struggled to remain upright against the sudden gust.

And then it stopped, holding its breath once more. Even the distant dripping in the stone seemed to stop.

Then: a low, thrilled chuckle. Shannon's mirthless, sarcastic laugh but braided with an old crone's cackle. A dichotomy of emotion, as the voice of some foreign-born hag lilted near my right shoulder.

"He thinks the coins aren't his, but still he wishes to give them away. And for me to take them! Such a fool, still playing at being a hyena when he's already proven himself the wolf; a devourer if ever there were one."

The title was bestowed upon me with everything but care. A hand pressed up the front of my shirt, but the middle finger was bisected by a razor-sharp talon that teased at my sternum, eager to flay and pierce my chest open with the merest of pressure.

"Say their names, then—the ones whose coins you want to give," offered Allen's lazy voice, the sudden scent of weed and incense filling my sinuses.

"My mother—," I started before the claw tapped my sternum chidingly.

"No, no, no, little wolf," my mother's voice whined in the same way it had when I disappointed her. Her voice hit me in the center of my being, a dropped anvil that caved me in around it. Even so I didn't have the energy to react to the pain the voice brought me. "Her passing gave you a coin, but whose coin is it?"

It dawned on me then. I'd been thinking of the coins as being not mine, but someone else's. But they were mine. They were part of me.

"Yes," Alicia's voice purred. "The child begins to understand."

The claw teased my flesh, eager for blood. Its tip stopped at the bottom of my solar plexus, waiting to push up and into my waiting chest cavity at the merest suggestion of permission.

"Let's count them, then," Theo offered, with mock encouragement. Always the helpful one. Always the shield I needed. "One by one."

My throat was dry. The words scraped on the way out, working around the foreign bodies that had invaded my heart like metallic slivers of sadness and hate and irreparable harm.

"Gold," I said, wincing. "I got it the night… the night I lost my innocence. Not sex. Not her body. The moment after—when I realized the peace I felt wouldn't last—"

The pain of the talon shearing my flesh and pushing into my waiting innards was sudden, even if it was expected. My body instinctively tried to jerk away from the invader, but the darkness-dweller held me steadfast as it fished around inside my abdomen, weaving its way past my other organs to seek the coin purse that my heart had become.

I might have cried out. I might have screamed. But, if I am to be honest in these pages as I have labored so far to be, I can't even recall making a solitary whimper.

But I do remember the delighted sigh that rippled through the cave, a chorus of dozens of mouths all exhaling at once. The breathy noise was thick with ecstasy and release. Every part of the creature's form that made contact with my body shuddered, a thunderous and yet still muted laugh bellowing around me. The sound echoed more in my ears than it did against the walls.

"Another joke for us, little canine?" teased a woman's voice. Sultry, carnal, and cruelly amused. Who was that? "Maybe you could've been a hyena after all!"

"What—? The night I lost my virginity—" I fell short as the digits of the limb—I struggled to think of it as a hand—crept over the flesh of my heart in a way that could only be called threatening.

"There was no gold in that night's activities, boy," Alicia's voice cut in, dripping with derision, as if she were mocking how clumsy and fleeting it had been.

"That night, you only gained silver. The night you wore love's costume and took more than you would ever give in return."

The claw—or whatever the knot of blades and digits could be called—jerked free from my chest.

Light. Sudden and searing. Not illumination, not clarity. Just pressure. Light without warmth, without color. It revealed nothing. It devoured sight. In the middle of that blinding nothing, something darker still emerged. Inky blackness, shaped like claws, held aloft a single, gleaming silver coin.

Not gold.

Silver.

And it was at that moment understood.

Not what I thought I'd earned. Not some noble shedding of innocence when I lost my virginity.

No.

She… Alicia had wanted love. Deserved love. And I gave her a performance. Affection, yes. Desire, sure. But not love. Not the kind she was giving me. Not the kind she needed. I'd let her believe in something deeper than I could reach. And still I'd taken. Still I'd held her. Still I'd smiled. That was the moment. Not when I lost something, but when I let her lose it.

The trust. The illusion. The hope.

Not gold, no. Never gold.

Silver. It was silver for betrayal.

I could almost hear The Oracle's needle-toothed grin in the

dark. The silver glinted once more before vanishing back into the dark, hidden away somewhere in the depths of the beast's horrid mass. A hiss of breath passed over my shoulder like steam through a cracked bathroom door.

"But…" I said, my voice unable to muster any real strength in my objection, "The tablet? The poem. It turned gold after that night. After… after her."

A pause. A beat of stillness so total it felt like the cave had stopped existing. Had I passed out standing there?

"Oh, little wolf. You still think the stone tells the truth?"

The awful, mocking laugh that danced around me felt like a thousand prickling stab wounds. A single whisper broke off from the others, slithering like silk down my spine.

"It shows you what you believe you know. Not what is, only what you think is."

My stomach turned. The cave felt smaller again, the air thick and fetid. My memories warped in my mind. Had the glow been gold, truly? Or had I just seen what I needed to justify it all?

"You knew what you wanted it to mean," offered Alicia's voice, scathing and maternal at the same time. "So that's what it became. A child's trick, played by a boy desperate to matter."

"You assigned the color," said my father's tone, clipped and cold. "The poem only reflects."

"Gold is precious," Shannon whispered now, softer than the others, and tinged with hurt.

"But you gave me silver," Alicia finished with an accusing tone that made a stone form in the pit of my stomach.

I swallowed, and this time, it felt as if the claw truly sliced into me as it explored for the slivers embedded in my heart.

I had come to this place certain of my understanding. But now, I wasn't sure I had known anything at all. When the claw retracted this time it held a golden coin that shone with all the light of the rising sun.

I blinked at it. The brightness was blinding. It was too bright. It didn't belong in this dead place. It didn't belong to the moment I thought it did.

Because I hadn't felt anything close to light that night on The Rock. No clarity. No revelation. Just noise and skin and confusion.

But this… this gold shimmered with something heavier.

"Not hers," I whispered, almost to myself. "It wasn't Alicia."

A breath stirred from the dark. No answer. No correction. But no denial either.

"It was my mom," I said, barely able to get the words out. "It was… when she died. That was the gold coin."

The golden light didn't change, but something inside me did. Like a key turning. Like a broken bone held in place with tightened muscles finally admitting to not being whole.

Because I remembered now. Not just the day she died. But the silence that followed. The unbearable quiet of a world without her voice. How everything had seemed too loud and too distant at once. How nothing had tasted right, how time had moved wrong.

How that was the moment I knew I wouldn't be okay again.

Not really.

"Gold for grief," I said. "For the first thing I ever lost that I couldn't get back. For the part of me that went with her."

The Oracle said nothing. The coin pulsed once in the

darkness. And I stood there, gutted and breathless, knowing that what I thought was love had only ever been mourning in disguise. Then the golden coin disappeared into the dark with a soft chime like a funeral bell.

Silence swelled again. Not peace, no, just that awful pressure of breathless space. I hadn't noticed I was crying until the tears reached my lips, bitter and useless. My throat burned, but I didn't sob. I couldn't. I didn't have that part of myself anymore.

Something clattered just beyond the edge of my hearing. Metal on stone.

Then: a sharp click.

And the claw returned, burying into me and pulling free in one sudden motion that left me on the verge of vomiting into the void that surrounded me.

Iron.

Heavy, dull, rusted. It gleamed the orange-red of a blood-rusted blade. It didn't shimmer; it was too harsh of a hue for that. Iron didn't ask to be claimed. It announced itself.

I stared at it for a long moment, my breath shallow.

"I know what that one is," I said flatly.

No voice interrupted. No mockery came. Even The Oracle's malice seemed to wait.

"I slept with her," I said, "because it was easier than facing myself. I wanted to bury the guilt, the anger. Drown it. Smother it. And I used Shannon to do it."

I swallowed against the rising taste of bile.

"I killed the part of me that still hesitated—the enemy that would've let me die if I didn't do what was needed. The part that would've stopped to ask who I was hurting. I let it die. On purpose."

The claw twitched slightly, almost like a nod. The iron coin's violent hue flickered, just once, like a drop of blood catching light, and then sank backward into the darkness to join the others.

"That one wasn't forged by loss," Shannon whispered into my right ear, her voice spitting venom. "It was forged by choice. A choice you made."

The Oracle finally stirred, no words, just a long exhale that sounded like wind through bone. It felt approving, as if the evil creature had made me more like it, if only slightly.

Iron was not grief.

Iron was cruelty in the shape of survival.

Iron was doing what had to be done, no matter who you hurt.

Iron you could only get if you made yourself the villain of your own story.

But the claw wasn't done.

This time, it didn't reach for me. It simply hovered. Waiting in the darkness beyond sight, but not beyond being.

Something shifted inside my chest. Not a physical pain, not even a memory, just an ache. A familiar emptiness. The kind you stop noticing after carrying it long enough.

I knew what I needed to do. I drove my own hand into the gaping wound of my chest. The warm gore squished around my hand as I felt around, feeling my thundering heart bump into my knuckles in a rhythmic pulse: *ba-dump, da-bump, ba-dump.* My fingers felt over the edges of two coins, side-by-side and protruding from the pulsing flesh and gripped them with my forefinger and thumb.

I pulled them free and held them before my face, dripping with blood and glowing the dullest of all the coins, even with their lights combined.

Not bright. Not proud.

Copper.

Their dull red-brown shimmer was lifeless, like the blood that sizzled and dried to their surface.

And I knew. I knew before a single voice spoke.

"I didn't even see it when it happened," I murmured, barely more than a breath. "Not until it was too late."

The Oracle waited patiently, hand still waiting in that endless expanse of black. It was still now. Listening.

"When Aiden died, I wasn't the only one who broke. Alicia…" I paused, eyes stinging. "She looked at me differently after that. Not all at once. But it started that night."

The coins hovered closer. I didn't try to touch them.

"She didn't blame me," I said. "Not outright. But she knew that I let him die, that I let him fall over that edge. That's when her love for me… it died."

Alicia's voice whispered in my ear, as soft a as a summer breeze, "Copper… from a loved one's eyes…"

"I… I do love her, and I ruined it when I didn't save him. She'll never love me again."

"She saw what you allowed," my own voice accused me in that awful mimicry The Oracle used. "And what you let yourself become after."

I nodded. "That's what the copper coins are. Not guilt. Not

grief. It's… absence. The part of me that still believed I could be loved without consequence."

I lowered the coins to where I knew the clawed hand waited. The two coins clinked softly against the reptilian flesh, then pulled apart, one retreating left, the other right, into the invisible jaws of The Oracle.

Gone. All five.

Silver, gold, iron, and two coppers.

Each a different demise; each one a smaller death of my own. I stood in the darkness, lingering in silence as I felt my unharmed chest with surprisingly calm fingers. I was alone and unmaimed. No claws. No whispers. No breath against my neck.

Just me. And the weight of the five coins that weren't in my pocket but were still deep inside of me, lodged behind my ribs. Rusted keys in forgotten locks I'd never wanted to open. The coins would never leave me; they would be in my heart for the rest of my days, I knew.

I swallowed hard and asked the question that had haunted me from the moment I stepped from this place with an answer no one truly wanted.

"Will you change my fate now?"

Silence.

Then a sound like something ancient unfolding. A flex of wet wings, or glaciers cracking under the weight of something older than time itself.

A laugh, low and indulgent, pealed out from the ink-stained dark. Not cruel, no, it was so much worse than cruel. The Oracle was amused with me.

"Oh, little wolf," The Oracle purred, its voice so rich with condescension I could feel it slick my skin like oil. But for the first time, I didn't know the voice at all. "Still clinging to the idea that I ever had such power?"

"You… you promised," I said, though even as I said it, the words felt small in my mouth.

"I did nothing of the sort," it replied, now shifting with a dry rasp of scales in the darkness. Its true voice seemed so small when compared to its imagined scale of mass. "You came to me begging for a change. And I gave you the opportunity to change. That's all I've ever offered anyone. That's all anyone can ever offer. The rest, you carved into your own flesh."

The cave pulsed with heat, though it was not a comforting warmth. It was much closer to the imposing hatred of a desert sun and the diamond-crafting pressure of unyielding earth.

"You changed your fate the moment you chose to seek those accursed coins; the moment you decided to return," it said. "The moment you walked through that first lie. Every coin you earned wasn't a curse I gave you—it was a truth you uncovered about yourself, little wolf. You did all of this to yourself."

I said nothing. I couldn't.

"You want salvation? You want redemption?" The Oracle asked, voice splitting into dozens of layered tones again. Alicia's sharpness, Shannon's hurt, my father's disappointment, even my own voice, warped and broken. "Then take it. Be the man you are. Or kill him and become something else. That is not my business to worry myself over."

I finally found my voice. "And what happens if I don't?"

The air drew taut, pulled tight like a razor-sharp string on the verge of snapping.

"Then you rot," The Oracle said, gentle as a lullaby. "Like all the others who came before you. Not damned. Not saved. Just… another among the forgotten."

A long pause followed. Some part of me wanted to lash out, but I refused to give the creature the satisfaction.

Then, softer and closer than even Alicia had ever been, it whispered in my own voice: "The only fate left to you, wolfling… is the one you decide you're willing to endure."

When I broke back into the clearing outside the cave, the sun was high overhead and I knew somewhere in my heart the price to forgo my death was paid in full and that it was up to me to be the person I wish I had been to begin with. So, I asked myself a question that sat even more bitter on my tongue than the one I asked that damned being: *Who am I going to become now that I have burned every bridge I've built with the Cavers?*

And so, I walked through that clearing, the sun warming my cave-cooled skin. I didn't run from my actions, though I left them behind me. But, instead, I struggled forward—toward the man I might still become. Because that was the only answer I could form to that most bitter of questions.

What Five Coins Bought Him:
Theo

I watched Will feed the last of his bags into the truck, the morning light catching motes of dust in the cab. They floated lazily but still carried a weight of finality. I couldn't quite articulate the feeling of the meeting at that moment, but now I would call it a somber parting. Like an echo returned too many times, refusing to give up the ghost of the speaker's voice.

Will moved slowly, like each motion cost him something unspeakable and leaving wasn't so much a choice he wanted, but a scrabbling reach for survival. I stood by his truck's open driver's side door, the brim of my ballcap low over my eyes to cut off any potential of eye contact at the moment. I held a stack of letters he'd pressed me into distributing; another layer of the echo bouncing back with a weaker and weaker ringing.

Four envelopes, each with a name scrawled in Will's jagged handwriting. They felt light in weight but heavy in importance. My thumb worried at the corner of the top one, Alicia's name written ever so slightly neater than the others. The paper was already softening under the minute sweat of my grip.

"You sure you can't do this yourself?" I asked, voice low. It wasn't meant to be accusatory, I was just wrung out. It was the exhaustion that had settled on all five of us after what had happened—what he did to all of us.

When I lifted my eyes from under the cap's bill Will refused to meet my eyes as he answered. He just nodded at the letters in my hands as he confessed, "It's better this way. After everything with Alicia and Shannon… I wouldn't know how to face them." He trailed off, swallowing hard. His gaze wandered to the cracked leather of the steering wheel, still too ashamed to meet my own. His fingers drummed once, restless, on the door frame as he tried to find a polite way to extricate himself from an already doomed situation.

I opened my mouth, then shut it. I wanted to tell him how cowardly it was, how I had expected better of him. But the word felt cruel in my throat, so I swallowed them back down and let silence be the jury of his actions.

Maybe it was cowardly. But maybe I understood, too. I even knew then that the wounds were too raw, for all of us, but that he also had the guilt in his heart of being the one that held the dagger.

Before he could climb in, I grabbed him by the shoulder and pulled him into a hug. I was angry, yes, but I wasn't going to let my best friend of four years leave without embracing him. He went stiff for half a second, more deer than wolf, then slumped against me. I felt his duffel bag straps digging into his back, smelling the mix of engine oil laced exhaust and cheap laundry detergent on his shirt. My eyes burned but I bit the urge to cry back.

"You've got a friend in me, no matter how far your dumbass runs," I murmured. My voice stayed steady, but I squeezed tighter so he'd feel what I couldn't say: I was angry, but I loved him like a sibling my parents had never given me.

He let out a shaky breath that might have been a laugh. When he stepped back, there was a shine in his eyes he tried to rub away with the heel of his hand. "I don't deserve a friend that good," he said, attempting a grin. It faltered, turning into a grimace. "But thank you."

The *crunch-grind-pop* sound of his dad pulling the rental moving truck out of the driveway felt like the crinkling of a tapestry that the five of us had worked too hard on for too long. The noise seemed to remind him of his purpose, and some lingering resistance to leaving gave way to the clockwork of his prior choices.

He climbed into his beat-up little truck and slammed the door—not with any particular emotion, just the way you had to close truck doors like his. The engine coughed to an unsteady life. I took a step back, letters clutched in both hands now. Will's window rolled down with a squeal. He looked at me once more. "I—" he began, then just shook his head. "Take care, Theo."

I nodded. Sometimes that's all you can do, just accept what you can't change. He put the truck in gear, and the tires crunched over the gravel as he pulled away, adding even more damage to our tapestry. I watched him go until the taillights disappeared around the bend at the end of our street.

The morning was quiet again. His dust hung in the air longer than I thought possible. I stood there with that little bundle of paper promises in my hands, feeling the weight of all he couldn't say. One by one, I shuffled through them. Alicia. Allen. Shannon. And one with my own name on it. I pressed that last one to the back of the stack and drew a long breath. There would be time for that later. Right now, I had deliveries to make.

Alicia would be my first stop, the first to receive her official parting. The walk I had taken so many times, which took ten minutes on a slow day, now dragged on for half an hour. The walk meandered here, lingered there, and

The sun had fully broken the horizon and was peeking over the trees that framed our neighborhood. By the time I got to her house I could feel the sun's white glare on the back of my arms, and I found her on the front porch digging splinters out of the rail with her thumb.

She straightened when she saw me rounding the walk. Alicia was always hard to read—today even more so. Her face was pale, freckled skin gone ashen and the color of a bruised apple under the eyes, but her posture was prim and still. "He's gone," she said softly. Not a question. She could always see the truth before it was spoken.

I swallowed. "He left this for you." I held out the envelope. My hands were dirty with the road dust from leaning on his truck, and I wished I'd washed them first.

Alicia's fingers hovered a second before taking the letter. She didn't invite me in, and I didn't expect her to. I just waited while she slid a fingernail under the flap and drew out the folded page inside. A single sheet to break her away from his ongoing story.

She unfolded the letter with delicate precision, the way you might unearth something fragile. Then she read. Her eyes moved left to right, line by line, her lips parted but no sound coming out. I stood still, listening to the far-off buzz of cicadas and the creak of the loose porch board under my foot. In that hush I could almost hear Will's voice in the back of my mind, saying what she was seeing on the page.

Alicia,

I'm writing this because I need you to know: I see it now. All of it. I see what I took from you. Not just your trust. Not just your love. I took the part of you that still believed I could be good.

And honestly, Alley-Cat, I fucked up. I slept with Shannon. I wanted you to hear it from me first. But I need you to know that I knew it would break you—and I did it anyway. I told myself it wasn't to hurt you, just to prove I was already beyond fixing. It was a lie, and it worked. You didn't deserve to be part of that.

I don't expect you to forgive me. I wouldn't forgive me.

You were the only thing in my life that made me want to stop running. You saw the worst parts of me and didn't look away. That scared me more than anything that horrid beast ever said.

I'm moving with my dad, back west a bit, going to college. Maybe start a cave diving or spelunking team over there, who knows? But...

I won't be coming back. I doubt you'd want me to after this. But if there's any part of you that still thinks of me, I hope it's the night we spent in the tent. Your hand in mine. The quiet. That was real. It was the only thing that felt untouched by the fucking cave.

You taught me that being known doesn't have to be a threat. That maybe I could've been more than what I was, even if I died young.

I'm trying to become someone who wouldn't do what I did. Not for you. For me.

But if that's not enough, I understand.

Goodbye, Alicia.

-W.

She didn't cry, not while I was standing there. But I saw her jaw tremble as she refolded the letter and tucked it into its envelope. She held it against her chest like something precious and poisonous all at once. Tears shone in her eyes but they didn't spill. Alicia was too proud for that. Or maybe too stubborn? Who am I to say which it was.

I had to force words out of my throat. "Ali…" I began, not even sure what I meant to offer. Apology? Comfort? None of it would be enough.

She closed her eyes and shook her head. A single tear escaped, tracing a line down her cheek. "I'm okay," she whispered, voice thin as paper.

She wasn't, though. We both knew it. But I didn't argue. I just nodded and stepped off the porch. My boots thumped on the hollow wood steps, a tired drumbeat of defeat.

Behind me, I heard the screen door open and close with a soft creak as Alicia retreated inside. I paused at the foot of the steps, looking back. Through the front window, I could just make out her silhouette sinking to the floor, clutching that letter in both hands.

I turned away. There was nothing left I could do for her right then. Not when I was carrying the source of our hurt in my pocket.

And, so, I headed off to Allen and Shannon's to deliver their pain next. During the stroll I sat on the roadside for a moment and pondered over my letter, considering if I should open it now so that I could share in their grief and understand their reactions better. I don't know how long I stayed there, eyes tracing over my own name inked onto the envelope like a dire warning of what lay beyond.

Finally, I decided against it and stood, continuing the slow march toward their siblings' home. When I finally reached their sturdy oak door, I gave it five rhythmic raps in the same way I always did. After a moment, Allen answered; eyes bloodshot and shadowed. He had a tired expression that went beyond being sleep-deprived and dipped into being haunted.

The living room behind him was dim, the TV off, an ashtray overflowing on the coffee table with his mom's favorite cigarette butts. He stepped out onto the porch with me, gently closing the door behind him as if not to wake something.

We stood there awkwardly. Allen managed a weary smile that didn't reach his eyes. "Figured I'd be seeing you," he said. "He's gone, huh?"

I nodded and held out the envelope with his name. Allen took it, turning it over once in his rough hands. I saw dirt under his nails, as if he'd been out back digging at the earth, searching for nothing but just trying to find something to do.

He sank down to sit on the top step, elbows on his knees, and opened the letter. I remained standing, one hand on the porch rail. Allen was usually the first to crack a joke in tense moments, but now he just pressed his lips together and started reading. The afternoon heat was coming on, and sweat darkened the back of his shirt. I watched a wasp circle lazily above the porch light as the thick silence of someone reading bad news settled in.

Allen,

You were always the one who showed up. When everyone else was too afraid or too angry or too tired, you were there: cracking a joke, passing the flashlight, keeping the silence from swallowing us whole.

I let that loyalty turn into something twisted. I leaned on you too hard. I let you defend me when I wasn't worth defending. I let you carry the weight of my silence, like it was your job to translate me to the others.

It wasn't. That was never fair.

I think about that a lot, how I made you the guy who had to choose between your friends and your conscience. And when everything went to hell, I left you in the fallout, pretending like walking away was cleaner than looking you in the eye.

I saw you slipping before I left. Not all at once—just in pieces. The way you started smoking more. The way your laugh got slower. Like you were trying to blur the edges so you didn't have to hold the whole shape of what I'd done.

You don't have to carry it anymore. None of it was yours to hold.

You were the best of us. Not because you were perfect, but because you were there. Steady. Honest. Human.

So let this letter be the thing that lifts it off your chest. I see you. I'm sorry I turned your loyalty into a burden.

Whatever you do next, I hope it's for you.

Thanks for being my friend, even when I didn't deserve it.

-W.

Allen blew out a long breath through his nose as he finished. He rubbed the back of his hand across his eyes, then pinched the bridge of his nose hard. For a long moment, he just sat there like that, face tilted down so I couldn't see what expression he wore.

I heard him sniff, then clear his throat. He folded the letter carefully along its original creases and looked up at me. His eyes were wet, but he tried for a smile anyway. "That dumbass," he said quietly, and a weak chuckle escaped him. "Takes off and leaves me with an apology I can't even reply to." I could see him reaching for a joke to tack on, failing to find it.

I let out a breath I hadn't realized I was holding. "Maybe it's better he put it in writing," I offered gently. "Will's never been great at goodbyes. You remember how he was when Alicia broke up with him."

Allen nodded, turning the folded paper over in his fingers. "Yeah. I guess… I guess we all got what we deserved, huh? One way or another." His voice cracked on the last words. Guilt clung on him, a second skin that weighed more than iron. I could see it clear as the day around me; he blamed himself for not saving us all from the impact of that horrible monster out in the woods.

I stepped over and sat down next to him on the step. The wood was hot from the sun, biting at me, even through my jeans. "None of us deserved this," I said, staring out at the empty street. "Not what we were told. Not what happened to Aiden. Not what happened after."

Allen's jaw tightened, and he looked away toward the yard, where a rusted swing set stood crooked in the grass. "Shannon's at The Rock," he murmured after a moment. Of course she was, where else would she be? "Took off this morning before I was even up. I'm guessing you've got one for her, too?"

I tapped the remaining two envelopes against my palm. "Yeah."

"Figures." Allen wiped his face roughly, smearing tears, sweat, and dirt across his cheeks. He stood, and I rose with him. "Better get it to her, then. Before she does something stupid out there." He tried to sound light, but his tone fell flat and grave. We both knew Shannon's worst impulses wouldn't be calmed by a letter.

I put a hand on his shoulder and gave it a squeeze. "You gonna be alright?"

He nodded vaguely. "Eventually," he said. "Don't worry about me. Just… go to her."

I left him on that porch, staring down at the letter in his hands, trying to wring more out of it if he just squeezed hard enough. As I headed down the street, I heard the creak of the screen door opening again and Allen's voice, low: "Hey, Theo."

I paused, looking back over my shoulder. He stood in the doorway, one hand braced on the frame. "Thank you," he said. Two simple words, heavy with everything else he meant.

I gave him a short nod, turned, and walked on. The trip through the woods blurred by, despite my feet feeling leaden and my pace languishing. It was the only trip that took less time than normal. I don't remember rushing, but the evidence that I had was there.

The Rock sat at the edge of the woods, a hulking limestone boulder etched with decades of teenage promises and betrayals.

By the time I reached the clearing, the sun was leaning into the afternoon, throwing narrow shadows around the trees. I spotted Shannon immediately—perched atop the stone that once seemed much more massive, one knee drawn up to her chest. Her fiery hair was pulled into a messy ponytail, and in her hand a rusty flathead screwdriver glinted, catching the light and turning it blood-orange hued. She was twirling it idly, a clear warning of her intent upon that grief-riddled stage.

Climbing up, I felt a familiar tightness in my chest. It happened every time I approached her, ever since the first time we'd kissed on this very rock last fall. For a few short weeks, we'd tried to be something more to each other. I remembered her laughter echoing against the stone, the warmth of her hand in mine as we lay on its sunbaked surface, naming cloud shapes like we were still little kids. But grief and guilt have a way of eating away at anything good. We drifted apart before we ever really came together. By the winter, whatever we'd had was gone to frost.

She heard me coming and looked over her shoulder. Her eyes were red-rimmed but dry. "So," she called out, voice flat, "he really did it. Will's gone?"

I hauled myself up the last bit of stone and stood a few feet from her. She was sitting beside the section of rock where one particular name waited, carved with that very screwdriver.

WILLIAM 2001

It still lay there; jagged letters made up of lines deep and sure.

Just mere feet away another name lay with a heavy scratch from Shannon's own hands. A name that was better off forgotten. One that Will hadn't said since he understood the importance of the line through it.

But, for now, Will's name was still intact.

Shannon tapped the screwdriver against the rock, right next to Will's letters: *clink, clink, clink.* Rust on stone, one decaying modernity and the other steadfast history. "He didn't even say goodbye," she said. Her knuckles were white around the handle, but there were no emotions on display.

I crouched down on the rock a couple feet away, balancing with one hand. I slid Will's final letter—her letter—out of my pocket and held it out. "I think *this* is his goodbye."

She stared at the envelope like it was a rabid animal, waiting to strike the moment she moved. She didn't reach for it. "Read it to me," she said.

I hesitated. "Shannon, it's probably personal—"

She cut me off with a sharp laugh. "Personal?" Her eyes flashed, and for a second, I saw hurt crack through the veneer of emerald anger, acting as a backlight to her barely contained fury. "I fucked him, Theo. I straddled him, rode him, and let him finish in me. That *personal* enough for you? There's nothing in that letter more personal than that, so fucking read it."

A hot spike of anger lanced through me suddenly, so fast I almost rocked back. I could see, in my mind, the two of them together in her dark basement, trying to smooth out their hurt and need with a passion I wanted to give. Shannon's pain was lashing out at both of us, and I wouldn't add mine to it. My hands curled against the stone, but I swallowed it down. Soon I had returned to my cool indifference and could focus on helping Shannon through this.

I cleared my throat and unfolded the letter. She turned her face away, eyes on the trees, as if she couldn't stand to watch me read it. So, I steadied myself and gave voice to Will's words, right there on The Rock where we'd all sworn oaths, he ended up breaking.

Shannon,

I won't dance around it. What I did was cruel.

You didn't ask to carry my collapse, but I dropped the whole damn weight on you anyway. I looked you in the eyes and made you think it meant something, and maybe some part of it did, but not the part you deserved.

You weren't a shortcut to forget Alicia. You weren't a placeholder. You were yourself, and I saw that. I just wasn't strong enough to handle it the way you deserved.

I don't expect kindness from you, or even a memory of the better me. If you Scratch me from The Rock, I won't blame you; it might be the right thing. But I hope, quietly and selfishly, that if it comes to that, you're the one carving in the final line. You more than anyone else deserve to banish me.

I keep replaying the basement— the way the smoke curled in the lamplight, how your laugh cracked when I called myself a washed-out wolf. I remember you tugging my sleeve and saying, "Maybe let the deer stop running for once." You were talking about yourself more than me, and I was too busy drowning out my own issues to hear or understand what you meant. But I think I get it now. You wanted me to catch you, huh?

You once said real loyalty is guarding the soft parts of a friend when they're too tired to guard them themselves. You did that for me on the creek bank, when the police lights turned Aiden's blood into strobing pools of darkness and everyone else turned away, unable to look at me. I paid you back by proving every fear you'd ever had about being a second choice.

But, if there's a night somewhere in your mind that still holds that better me, I hope it's the fire-ring at Shit Creek when you called me "Mad-wolf". I remember watching the sparks climbing into the dark, letting the name settle into my heart, right next to those damn coins. It was the perfect name for me, even then.

You matter, Shannon. You always did. And you deserved much better than this, but all I have left is to say it: I'm sorry.1

-W.

The letter fluttered a little in my hands as I finished reading—the breeze had picked up, or maybe I was shaking. Shannon stayed quiet through the whole thing. When I finally glanced at her, she was squeezing her eyes shut, tears leaking out the sides and tracing slow, mascara-black lines down her cheeks.

I folded the letter back up as neatly as I could and returned it to its flip-top prison. Without a word, I set it down on the rock beside her, anchoring it with the handle of her screwdriver so the wind wouldn't take it. I pushed myself upright, knees popping after crouching so long, and turned to go.

I'd made it two steps when her voice came, small and raw: "Theo?"

I paused, my back to her. "Yeah?"

Her breath hitched. "Should I do it?"

I knew exactly what she meant. I looked over my shoulder and found her staring at Will's name on the rock, screwdriver clutched to her chest now, the letter wrapped around the handle in her iron-tight grip. In that dying light, she was still beautiful, even with a mask of grief and fury settled over her face. I saw it there, in her eyes. I knew it long ago, but sitting there I could see it. She loved him still, even after what he did.

My throat tightened. Part of me wanted to tell her yes. Yes, scratch his name out, make him a ghost like Aiden. He'd earned it for himself. But when I opened my mouth, the words that came were gentle. "He's done everything to deserve it," I said, each word measured. "Even so… I can't bring myself to hate him for it." I felt my chest ache as I admitted it. "You do what you think is right, Firetwig."

Shannon let out a breath like a sob. I don't know if it was relief or resignation. I didn't wait to see what she would do. I climbed back down off The Rock, leaving her alone in the midday glow of a thick forest. She had a choice to make.

When I emerged from the woods I went to my car, pulled out of my drive way, and drove through the tree-shaded backroads that stretched out into oblivion in every direction that wasn't toward the larger city down the interstate. As I weaved in and out of those backroads I kept glancing over at the letter—my letter—in the passenger seat.

Twice I stopped to read it.

The first was in the parking lot of a tiny church that easily had more tombstones in its cemetery than attendees in the past fifteen years. I sat in that parking lot and flipped the letter over in my hand, working myself up to open it. But I couldn't. So, I tossed it back in the passenger seat and pulled out of the church.

The second was in the small gravel lot behind The Wagon Wheel. How many times had we eaten here after school? How many times had Will stolen fries from my plate while quoting John Stuart Mill to justify it? How could I find a better place than this that wasn't tied to the machinations of that horrid creature?

I went in and ordered an early dinner, bouncing the letter against the table as I waited for my food and the right time to open it. I finished the meal and never found that time, so I left.

Twilight had firmly settled by the time I pulled into my driveway. I stepped through my front door. The house was still; Dad's missing car meant that he was probably out for the whole night, finally trying to find a connection to mend his heart after all these years, and failing horribly at it. I flicked on a lamp in the living room. Its yellow glow fell over the same old couch and the stack of unopened mail on the side table. Everything ordinary, in its place. And yet nothing felt the same.

I lingered in the doorway of our small dining room, eyes drawn to the empty chair at the head of the table. Mom's chair. The ache of her absence swelled up so sudden that I had to reach out to stabilize myself. It still happened like that, the grief sneaking up like a thief in the dark.

Will was her favorite, for the short time she knew him. She'd never get to know his teenage-philosophical stage or how his time with the Cavers ended. Maybe that was a mercy.

I made my way to my bedroom, the last envelope held tight in my hand. The floorboards creaked under me in the hall. In my room, I didn't bother with the overhead light; I just sat on the edge of my bed in the bluish glow from the streetlamp outside. The crickets were loud tonight. Or maybe I was just too quiet.

For a long moment I stared at my name on the envelope, written in Will's sloppy marker scratch. I wasn't sure I wanted to know what he'd said to me. I was so angry at him. Angry about what he'd done to our friends. Angry for running away. Part of me even blamed him for Aiden, for all the darkness that had crept into our lives after the falls. But another part of me just… missed my friend. The friend who had crawled through hellish caves with me, who had waxed poetic about whatever stupid philosophy he had recently picked up on, who had once looked at the stars with the same wonder I did.

My chest felt tight as I finally tore the envelope open and

smoothed out the pages. In the dim light, I began to read Will's farewell to me.

Theo,

I've never told you this, but I looked up to you more than anyone else in the group. You brought meaning to what we did. You made it feel like something bigger than a game or a dare. You made it sacred.

I still hear your voice by the creek, your dad's old oil lantern popping while you read those childish ghost stories about voice stealing rocks and gatekeepers in gray while the rest of us drank our spirits and mocked how serious you were.

And I broke it.

I know you better than I let on. If I had come to you, really told you what was happening, you would've tried to forgive me. Maybe you still would. But I can't let you do that, not before I've even begun to earn it.

There are things I have to face alone: the cave, that dark beast, myself. I can't keep dragging people in to carry pieces of what I should have held from the start. Especially not you. Not again.

I'm leaving—not to hide, but to rebuild. Slowly. Quietly. On my own.

If we meet again, I'll tell you everything. No riddles. No weight shifted onto someone else. Just the truth.

Until then, be well. Be better than we were. I already know you will be.

-W.

By the end, my hands were trembling. I closed my eyes, resting the letter on my knees. In the silence that followed, I could hear my own heartbeat in my ears, slow and heavy. There were tears on my face before I even felt them coming.

Will's words swirled in my mind. He believed I'd try to forgive him. That I'd succeed, given half a chance. He was right about the first part—I'd wanted to forgive him from the moment I realized what he'd done, even when it hurt. But whether I could or should was a different question.

I thought about Shannon on The Rock, screwdriver in hand. Alicia sank to the floor in her living room. Allen lighting another joint in his basement to numb the pain. We were all carrying pieces of what happened. We'd all paid for the question an irresponsible twelve-year-old had asked.

Out on the street, a pair of headlights swept past, then faded. I wiped my eyes with the heel of my palm and looked down at Will's letter again. My gaze caught on one line near the bottom, illuminated in the bluish light: If we meet again, I'll tell you everything.

He would. I believe that now. Will had run away rather than face us, but in his own broken way, he was trying to make things right. He was taking the darkness with him, so maybe we could heal.

I carefully refolded the letter and placed it back in its envelope. Then I sat there a while longer, hands on my knees, breathing in and out until the ache in my chest loosened. The anger in me had ebbed to embers. What remained was sorrow, and a fragile strand of hope for the boy who'd been my friend.

Maybe one day I could forgive Will. Maybe one day we'd all find a way out of the cave he'd dug for us. Until then, I would hold these letters, these truths, close. They were a map of everything we'd lost—and a compass, maybe, toward something like understanding.

Outside, the crickets kept on singing. I sat in their chorus of night sounds, quiet and still, and let the memories come and go like breaths. None of us were innocent, not anymore. But we were all still alive, and morning was on its way.

You have taken the first step into The Bitter Verse

You have heard The Bitter Question asked

You have seen the cost the answer carries

Now you will learn of what Remains

From the pages of The Bitter Remains...

Words From a Ghost

Will

I should have died my first death on my twenty-third birthday. Instead, I slowly died my second and third. I don't know when it started. Not exactly. There wasn't some moment where the sky split open or the world screamed that I wasn't welcome anymore. It was quieter than that. Slower. Like the edges of my life had started to fade—like a sun-bleached newspaper losing its words. And no one even noticed their slipping memories of me.

The first time someone forgot me, I thought they were joking. One of the frat bros I had to tutor through a natural science class. It was at a bar on the Saturday after my twenty-third birthday. I figured he was pretending not to know me as a prank or that he was drunker than he seemed. But it kept happening, and with people closer and closer to me. Bartenders. Neighbors. My Ph.D. advisor. My friends. My girlfriend.

That was the biggest shock. I had just put together what was happening and rushed over to her apartment to tell her. I walked in to find her curled up on the couch with someone else—laughing like she used to laugh with me. I said her name. She looked at me like I was a stranger. Not angry. Not scared. Just confused. Then she asked if I was her roommate's friend, and would I mind giving them some privacy. The guy she was with? He had been a friend of mine since freshman orientation. He looked at me like a complete stranger too.

I didn't even challenge them. I wasn't mad. It simply confirmed what I was piecing together.

After that, it got worse. And fast. People started to look through me. Literally. Like I was furniture or air. I stopped trying to talk to them. Stopped trying to make eye contact. The only thing worse than being invisible is realizing you're not even a ghost—you're a blank space everyone edits out of their story without meaning to. A character deleted from some historical tapestry.

I started taking what I needed. Food off tables. Clothes from lost and found bins. I figured if the world was done recognizing me, I didn't owe it anything either. But the forgetting wasn't the end. Not really. It was just a symptom. Something deeper was broken. And I needed to understand what it was—before I vanished entirely.

That's when I really gave up and went to the lake.

The first time? Only a couple of minutes before the screaming need of my lungs drove me back out of the water.

Second attempt? Two days. I lay there, at the bottom, waiting to sink into something final. It was a mixture of stomach cramps and the still crying lungs that drove me to the surface that time.

The third was the long one. I lost track of time, honestly. I know that winter had come and gone at least once, because I remember ice at least once.

My body still clawed for air, for warmth, for food. Still acted like I was human. The pain never stopped, but it eventually became a background hum compared to the way my mind turned over on itself over and over. Eventually I gave up. I would never know the peace of death.

Around then I felt a pulling, a tug on the frayed thread of whatever was left of "me". It drew me toward deep places that smelled like limestone and stale breath and forgotten secrets. Caves. Not the Oracle's cave. I didn't have anything left in me for that ancient entity. No, these caves were different. They held things that were…

Older.

Quieter.

More powerful.

It was in one of those caverns, where the Earth's held breath hung heavy, that a primordial being beckoned me. It did not speak, but pressed knowledge into me, forcing me to understand the cursed existence I would now endure for defying Fate. It revealed what humans were never meant to know, truths we were only ever meant to suspect.

It told me of the Three Deaths: The First Death, the Death of Breath; The Second Death, the Death of Name; The Third Death, the Death of Memory. Because of the Oracle, I had slipped past the first death. But the second and third had come for me anyway—slowly, but still far faster than they had any right to. And worst of all, I wasn't alone for this erasure.

The Fyrues were sent after me. They were decayed echoes of the Erinyes, long stripped of their original names and identity, only able to mimic their original purpose. They lingered on the edges of places I slept. Jealous whispers echoing in shadows, half lidded eyes leaking drifting ash, grinning mouths stitched shut while still leaking blood. They judged my every movement, pushing me to give up and accept oblivion.

They weren't acting on their own, of course. I had heard whispers deep in that cave, of a separate ancient being. One harsher, colder than the other. It carried the weight of an executioner's judgment. It was a force that no longer understood the difference between justice and a debt-ledger stained red with past due tithes. It wouldn't come to punish me, no. It would only come because I had taken more from reality than I should, and nothing more.

I didn't speak for a long time after that. Just wandered. Lingered on the edge of towns where no one knew me anyway, like that would make it hurt less to be ignored. I followed rivers like they might lead somewhere sacred, to caves with different answers. Even to somewhere cursed.

Eventually, I found myself drifting back to civilization. Not for any noble reason. Just the gravity of convenience. I was hungry. Cold. At some point—when I was too tired to keep moving through a hollow life, too empty to keep looking for answers—I just sat down and wrote my story. I copied it using some old library xerox. I went to places where a stack of papers would be read and left those copies to be found. Spread the story out like spores from some ancient fungus.

Like I mattered. But I wasn't a man anymore. Just an absence in reality. A blank space where I used to be.

So, unsurprisingly, a different type of gravity pulled me back home. Not to my house. It had new owners. A nice couple who watched old movies with the curtains open. That didn't matter, really. I could knock on any door and walk in once it opened. But that house felt like a line I shouldn't cross—for my own well-being.

But I did go back to that little town that was ghosted by infrastructure, with more tombs than homes. I went to places that used to mean something to us: the gymnasium where our prom was held and forgotten; the old train-depot where Allen would drop off his weed to old hippies that were looking to relive their "good 'ol days"; the little church where we held too many funerals for a group of teenagers to need to attend. To the Wagon Wheel. Our diner. We used to eat there, back when we were all still real. Before the coins. Before the cave. Before I started to hollow out my insides for a place to store them.

I would just wait until some tasty food hit a table I was strolling past, then did what I always do now. Took a fry here. A ceramic bowl of corn there. People never noticed. Or if they did, they forgot by the time they realized what was happening. Just a ghost of anger and then nothing but a missing order of fried okra that the waitress must have forgotten.

By then I'd accepted it—everyone was gone. Or worse, they weren't gone, they just didn't remember I'd ever been there to begin with.

As I reached for a half-eaten sandwich on the plate of a curly-haired woman with her back to me, my hand was slapped—hard enough to sting.

I recoiled, startled—not by pain, but by *purposeful* contact. There is a difference when you accidentally graze an arm in a crowd, and when someone *means* to touch you. I hadn't felt that in years.

I looked at the hand first. unsure if I'd imagined it.

The sting.

The weight.

The way her fingers curled tight like a warning told me there was no mistake in the touch. Then I saw the shape of her shoulders.

The way she sat upright without tension, like someone who never stopped scanning the world for who might leave next. The oak-brown curl of her bun. Imperfect. Familiar. My gaze dropped back to the plate.

I had reached for her food. *Her* food.

Something ancient twisted in my chest.

Recognition. Guilt. Grief.

Like I had broken into a memory and found it still breathing.

She turned.

Her mouth opened slightly, breath catching.

Her eyes locked with mine.

And then she said my name.

My name.

Full of shocked recognition.

Like it still meant something.

Like *I* still meant something.

Alicia remembered me.

Subscribe to the official Bitter Verse website to stay up to date on release dates, product announcements, and exclusive worldbuilding information at:

https://www.thebitterverse.com/

Get connected to the Bitter Verse by joining the official Discord, where you can trade your theories, share fanart, and meet other Bitter Readers like you at:

https://discord.gg/8byDVf5r4S